Lord of the Underworld:
A Ransom & Fortune Adventure

Volume 4

Michelle Miles

Lord of the Underworld

A Ransom & Fortune Adventure, Volume 4
This title has never been published before and is a brand-new adventure.

Skye and Dane hurtle through space and time only to end up in a desert world resembling that of Ancient Egypt…but not. As they navigate the dry, dusty world in the aftermath of war, Dane is heralded as the Lord of the Underworld, a god resurrected as human and eerily like the Egyptian god, Osiris. The ancient inhabitants fear him, the pharaoh and his wife worship him, while Skye, with her flaming red hair, is branded a sorceress and sent to work in the blistering heat as a slave.

Dane must work his way back to her but is thwarted by factions he never expected and can't outmaneuver. And when a new enemy appears, their situation becomes the most dangerous yet.

Prologue
The Lion's Den

Present Day, Arlington, Virginia

It had been nearly two weeks since Nick Slaughter found Thomas and Harold and took them away from their hideout in rural Pennsylvania. Two weeks of shear hell trying to move equipment without anyone knowing they made their way from the underground bunker to the state-of-the-art building right in the heart of Arlington, Virginia. They were a block away from Goldenrod Research and Development.

The lion's den.

Thomas may as well hand himself over to Janus Force and be done with it. Being so close to the company made him nervous. It was only a matter of time before they would find them. Despite Nick's assurances they were safe there, Thomas wasn't so sure.

And Harold. He was another mystery. He wasn't sure how he even found Thomas and that was nerve-wracking enough. But the kid knew a lot about Ransom's time travel research. Much more than could be attributed to an eidetic memory.

Thomas didn't want to say he was suspicious of the kid, but all signs pointed to he was suspicious.

Nick and his team of ex-military super-agents had a building they wanted to use as their headquarters. The place was three stories with apartments on the top floor and all the equipment on the second. The first floor was off limits and guarded twenty-four hours a day. It was as if Nick expected trouble. Despite the heavy security, it didn't really put him at ease.

The only thing Thomas had no problem with was moving into the spacious one-bedroom apartment. It was fully furnished and definitely a step up from his crappy underground hideout. Even the kitchen was fully stocked with everything he could want. He had weekly grocery deliveries paid for by Nick's company. He had a cleaning lady who came by twice a week and not only tidied up but did his laundry.

Despite all the amenities and all the luxury, Thomas would rather work on his own equipment in his own lab without someone hovering over him all the time.

He poured his first cup of coffee of the day and made his way from his apartment. The second level workroom, as they called it, was nothing but a large room with low-wall cubicles and every piece of computer equipment they could find. No phones. When he got to the second floor, he found Harold was already there hooking up the rest of his equipment. Nick had spared no expense in buying whatever they needed to get Skye and Dane back home.

The equipment Thomas brought over had been set up in an area in the far corner. It looked sadly outdated next to Harold's shiny new equipment.

"Thomas, hey. Are you ready to bring them home?" Harold gave a wave when he saw him, his youthful face breaking into a smile. He sat behind his ultra-wide curved monitor that took up the whole desk, then typed away on the keyboard.

Thomas sipped his coffee with as much calm as he could muster watching him log into the computer. "Do you think it's that easy?"

"Well, no." Harold launched a program that sent rows of code scrolling up the screen.

"Because it's not," Thomas said. "It won't be. It's not like picking them up at the airport. We have to find them first and even when we do, there's a chance they could time travel again. My equipment is only good enough to find them."

What he didn't say was that his equipment wasn't good enough to bring them home.

"That's why I'm going to help you." Harold gave him a wide winning smile. He went back to typing away on the keyboard, the key strokes nothing but a hum. He was impressed with how fast the kid could type.

Thomas sighed. He sipped more coffee as he made his way over to his computer. The kid was hopeless. He didn't seem to understand the situation was dire and impossible at the same time. If he couldn't figure out how to get them home, then Skye and Dane would definitely be stuck in time forever. Eventually the little time bender would give out completely. It wasn't made to last forever.

Harold got to his feet and followed him to his desk. "I asked Nick to help with some other things."

That gave Thomas pause. "What other things?"

"You know…software things."

He stared at the kid as if he'd grown a second head. "You asked him for software? What kind of software?"

"It's in beta right now."

"That's not what I was asking."

"He said he could get it."

Thomas narrowed his eyes. "Get it from where?"

The kid swallowed hard. "Goldenrod."

The blood drained from his head in a whoosh. His knees gave out. He sank to his chair, his mug hitting the desk in front of him with a thump. A few drops of coffee sloshed over the rim.

"You sent Nick Slaughter to Goldenrod Research Technology."

"Did you know he used to be a SEAL? I understand he only hires former military. I think one of the guys used to be in the 82nd Airborne." Harold completely ignored him as he rattled off the random information.

"I don't care about that," Thomas snapped. "Please explain to me why you sent Nick Slaughter to Goldenrod for some beta software?"

"Because we need it," was his lame response.

Thomas stared at him a long moment. A beat of silence passed. "What is this software?"

"Something that was in development when I left there." He twisted a loose thread from the end of his shirt around his forefinger.

Thomas was perplexed. He'd worked with William Ransom on his time traveling device from the very beginning. They had developed software, yes, as a way to track the device when it was on and off. Somehow, though, he didn't think Harold was talking about that.

"I don't know of any beta software."

"It was still in development," he said again.

"Was? I thought you said it is?"

"Is," he corrected. "Anyway, Nick assured me he could get it."

Thomas rubbed his forehead, pinching the skin between his thumb and forefinger. "I don't understand what this has to do with Skye and Dane."

"It will help get them home."

"How?"

"You'll see." He wandered back to his desk and sat again. His fingers pounded the keyboard as if his life depended upon it.

Thomas had to admit his curiosity was piqued. He walked over and stood behind him, watching. On the screen, more strange lines of that code scrolled upward at a rapid pace.

"What are you doing?" Thomas asked.

"What I need to," was his only terse reply.

As he watched him, he suddenly realized Harold had hacked into a network. His gut twisted. He didn't want to know but at the same time, he had to know.

"Who are you hacking?"

"No one of importance." He was intently staring at the screen. He hit another keystroke and then enter. A second later, he yanked the thumb drive out of the computer and held it up. "Got it."

"Got what?"

"Exactly what I needed." And suddenly, he didn't sound like a kid anymore.

~ ⧗ ~

Four hours later, Nick stormed into the workroom, angry lines all over his face. He headed right for Harold. He saw him coming and pushed back from his chair. Before he could get to his feet, Nick was on him, grabbing him by the collar and jerking him upward. Fear etched on Harold's face.

"You little bastard. You sent us on a wild goose chase."

Thomas launched to his feet and hurried over. "Nick, let him go."

Nick's head swiveled in his direction. "You stay out of this."

"I needed a distraction," Harold said, his tone high-pitched and fearful. "I'm sorry. It was the only way I could get what I needed."

Nick jerked him closer to his face. "You used me and my men."

"I'm sorry," he whispered.

"What is going on?" Thomas asked.

Nick shoved Harold back into his chair. "He sent us to Goldenrod for nothing. We couldn't even get into the building before we were discovered. Several of my men are injured."

Suddenly, everything clicked inside Thomas as he stared, wide-eyed at Harold. "You hacked Janus Force at Goldenrod, didn't you?"

Harold held up the thumb drive. "And got exactly what I needed." He straightened his shirt with his other hand and looked a Nick. "I'm sorry I used you and your men that way, but I needed them to be focused on something other than their network."

"You little twit. We were nearly killed because of you." Anger creased Nick's face.

But Thomas was too busy thinking about what Harold had actually done. "You stole their software. Oh, god." His gut clenched as he sank into the nearest chair.

"I had to."

"Software? What software?" Nick glanced from Harold to Thomas, question on his fury lined face.

"I thought you said that's what he was retrieving?" Thomas asked Harold, thumbing in the direction of the irate soldier.

Harold's face flushed bright red. "I sort of lied about that, too."

Thomas groaned, put his head in his hands and leaned over, fighting the urge to throw up his coffee. His stomach was in a wild knot.

"You little son of a bitch," Nick said. "The next time you get the bright idea to lie and use me and my men will be the last time."

Before Harold could reply, Nick stomped out of the workroom, the door slamming closed behind him. Only the buzz of the overhead lights and the hum of the computers could be heard in the room. Finally, Thomas lifted his head and looked at Harold. His face had paled of color as he stared down at the thumb drive in his hand. Thomas rose from the chair and walked over. He put his hand on the kid's shoulder.

"Maybe you should tell me what this software is."

Harold glanced up at him, an excited gleam in his eyes. "It's the beta software that ties into the time bender wherever in time it is. Then, we can project a holographic image to communicate with them."

"You mean we can get them a message? Let them know we're working on getting them home?"

Harold nodded. "There's only one catch."

Thomas didn't like the sound of that. "What's that?"

"I need one more piece of equipment to make it work."

Nope, he didn't like the sound of that at all. "And I suppose this equipment is back at Goldenrod."

Again, Harold nodded, his youthful face beaming hope. Hope that Thomas would end up helping him. How could he say no? Skye was his friend. If Harold, his software and his equipment was the only way to do that, then he would have to say yes. Wouldn't he?

Thomas ran his hand through his hair and paced.

"I know exactly where it is," Harold said, sounding hopeful. "If I can get into the building, I can get it."

"How do you propose to do that?" Thomas wanted to know.

"I don't know yet." He glanced toward the door Nick slammed. "I was hoping to ask Nick and his men for help on that, too."

"That's out of the question. We'll have to come up with another idea."

"We?" Harold's brows rose to his hairline. "Are you helping me now?"

Thomas took a deep breath as he looked at the kid. He didn't really have a choice, did he? "Yep. I'm helping you now."

~ ⧗ ~

A few hours later, after they had brainstormed ideas on breaking into Goldenrod, Thomas returned to his apartment for dinner and Netflix binge watching.

As he popped his meal of mac and cheese into the microwave, a knock sounded on his door. When he opened it, Nick Slaughter stood on the other side.

"We need to talk."

Thomas waved him inside. "About what?"

"Harold." Nick paused in the middle of the living room, his hands on his waist as he looked toward the windows.

"What about him?"

"How well do you know him?" Nick asked.

He didn't like where this line of questioning was going. "I guess not that well. He found me at my hideout. He said he was on the time bender team at Goldenrod."

Nick turned to face him. "And you believed him?"

"There wasn't a reason not to. He knows a lot about the research. What's this about?"

"I'm not sure I trust him." Nick made his way to the kitchen. He pulled open the fridge and grabbed a beer.

"Look, Nick, the stunt he pulled today was inexcusable. But he's a kid. I'm not sure he knows any better."

He took a swig of the beer. "I did some checking. The information I found for Harold Ravenwood appears to be too perfect."

Thomas really didn't like where this was going at all. "You checked up on him?"

"I ran background checks on both of you."

"Without my permission?" Thomas asked.

"A necessary precaution if we're working together to bring home my colleague."

Dane may be his colleague, but Skye was Thomas's friend. He'd known her for years. He folded his arms over his chest as annoyance trickled through him. "I would have appreciated the head's up."

"I apologize for running the background without asking, but you have to understand my position." He took another healthy swig of the beer. "I have trust issues."

"Clearly."

"And today's little stunt doesn't help Harold's case. He's hiding something."

Thomas could agree with that. He sensed something was off about Harold for a while now but he hadn't put his finger on it. "Maybe he is. Maybe we all are. All I know is I can't get Skye and Dane home without him."

Nick narrowed his gaze. "Do you trust him?"

"I know you think he's up to no good, but the kid hasn't done anything to make me not trust him."

Nick raised an eyebrow. "Except lying to me and sending my men on a wild goose chase."

"Which was only to help Skye and Dane in the long run," Thomas pointed out. "The kid is brilliant. I watched him hack into Janus Force without even breaking a sweat."

"That's something else. How did he manage to hack into their system? With DARPA involved, that makes it a felony."

"Like I said, the kid is brilliant. I'll talk to him if you want."

"You should. Tell him one more misstep and he's out." He finished the beer, then placed the empty bottle on the counter.

"I'll keep a close eye on him."

"You better." He headed for the door. "Whatever this software is Harold stole, I hope it was worth it. I have two men down because of it."

"I haven't seen the software in action, but I understand it will help us communicate with them through the time bender."

"And then we can get them home?" Nick asked.

"That's the plan."

He paused at the door, gave Thomas a nod. "Good to hear. Night."

As the door closed behind him, the microwave dinged but Thomas had lost his appetite.

~ ⧗ ~

Charles Ridgewood paced the length of his office biting his thumbnail. It had been nearly two weeks since they returned from their experience at the Citadel. Two weeks of silence and nothing. Two weeks of no progress. He was no closer to finding Skye and Dane than he was when he arrived home with an injured Ark Crane. The time bender they'd used to get home had died the second they arrived. And the time travel ship—for lack of a better word—was out of juice. In order to power the vehicle, he needed a combination of hydrogen and plutonium and he was fresh out of both.

Meanwhile, everything was on hold. He'd failed to bring back Skye. Ark had failed to kill Dane. As long as that man lived and time traveled with her, he was a threat and he was her bodyguard. They needed to neutralize him as soon as possible.

But Ark was currently in recovery and not exactly up for time traveling or assassinating anyone. Which frustrated Charles to no end.

A frantic knock on his office door broke him out of his dismal thoughts. Before he could say anything, the door flew open. Leonard, his Chief Technology Officer, burst into the room, a panicked look on his stricken face.

"Sir, we have a problem."

"What is it?"

"We've been hacked."

"Bloody hell. Who? How?"

"Someone was able to break in through a backdoor on our network. We detected the breach earlier this morning. Whoever it was knew exactly where to hit us and how to get in," Leonard said.

"This morning? When?"

"Around 8."

"Son of a bitch. That's when we were hit by those intruders. They must have been a distraction." He sat, hard, in his chair. "What's the damage?"

Leonard held up a thumb drive. "This was plugged into the computer that was hacked. It's an EXE file for software still in development."

Charles stared at the USB, an overwhelming sense of dread pouring through him. "What's the software?"

"It's for virtual reality communication, sir."

He blinked surprise. "Why would they want that?"

"I don't know since it's useless without the VR goggles."

"We have VR goggles here?"

"I'm told the pair are made especially for this software."

"Who told you?"

"Lucy Wakefield."

Of course, she would know. A theoretical physicist, she was one of the remaining people on William's original team to develop and build the time bender. She would know about that sort of thing.

"Where are these VR goggles?" Charles asked.

"She said the last time she saw them they were in William's office, but she hasn't seen them since before he died," Leonard said.

Charles shot to his feet and glanced around. He'd taken up residence in William's office when he took over Goldenrod. "I'll start looking for it. In the meantime, make sure the network isn't breached again. And find out how that software works."

"I'm on it."

As Leonard left, Charles started his search for the VR goggles. He had to get his hands on them as quickly as possible. If there was a way to get to Skye and Dane, he wanted to be first.

Chapter 1
Leap Through Time

Traveling through time sucked. It was quite possibly the worst thing Skye had ever done. If they ever got home, she made a promise to herself she would never leave again.

"Can *we* go home now?"

Dane slipped his hand out of his pocket and brought out the small device that had become the bane of their existence. She was beginning to hate the little thing. He flicked it on with the tip of his thumb.

"We can try. That's all we can do."

They both peered down at the thing in his hand. "And if we end up somewhere else?" she asked.

He placed his warm fingers under her chin and tipped her head back. She looked up into his depthless green eyes. He cocked a grin at her.

"We stick together no matter what."

She nodded. "No matter what."

He wrapped an arm around her and pulled her close. She clasped his hand holding the device, her thumb hovering over the top of his. She kissed Dane's scruffy face. The prickly sensation of his cheek made her lips throb. "For luck."

He gave her a quick smile and together they pushed the button, leaving the Citadel behind. She hoped they would end up closer to home. But coming awake after the violence of falling through time made her groan.

Heat pounded through her as she peeled her eyes open and tried to focus on her surroundings. Above her, a brilliant blue cloudless sky. Somewhere nearby she could hear the soft lapping of water. Not like an ocean. More like that of a lake.

She flung out her arm to feel the ground next to her. Her hand plopped into cool water. She rolled over and peered through cattails.

Where had they ended up this time?

She sat up, glancing around looking for Dane but he was nowhere in sight. They had pushed the button together but that didn't mean they would end up together. They'd been separated before. It was never a good thing. Dane was her protector and the only one she really trusted. Hell, he was the only one along for the ride with her so she *had* to trust him.

Not that she had any reason not to trust him. In wintertime, he'd rescued her from the crazy tribesman who wanted to marry her and then sacrifice her. In the Citadel, he'd managed to keep her safe from Charles Ridgewood and whatever he was up to.

She thought of Ridgewood now, of the strange machine he'd disappeared in, and wondered if he would be back. He seemed desperate to take her back with him. She had no idea what he wanted from her or why.

"Dane?"

She kept her voice low in case there were natives who wanted to do her harm. After everything they had been through, she'd learned to always stay on her guard. In the distance, she could hear a rhythmic thumping that sounded like a drum. She got to her knees and peered over the tops of the cattails.

Calm, blue water stretched between her and the other side of the river. On the opposite shore, she could see a processional. In the lead, a man banging a drum in a *thump, thump, thump.* Behind him, two men dressed in long scarlet colored robes, sandals, and a thick golden choker around their neck. Each wore a tall square-shaped headdress and carried a long pole with a red and gold banner flapping in the wind. Painted in the center of each banner was the silhouette of what reminded her of an Anubis.

Behind the two men, three women. All dressed in opaque flowing gowns in various earth-tone colors of red, orange, gold. The woman in the center wore black and had her head bowed in grief, her dark hair covered in jewels dripping down her back. Behind her, the four men carried what looked like a crude stretcher with a body swathed in gauze. Behind them, more men armed with swords and spears.

It was a funeral procession and, by the looks of it, the deceased had been someone important. She kneeled there on the edge of the water, watching as they made their way along the bank of the river. She leaned forward through the cattails to see they were headed toward a large stone temple carved into the side of the mountain. No doubt a tomb.

Fascinating.

Had they somehow landed in Ancient Egypt? If their time traveling history was any indication, it could be another alternate universe like the Citadel. Remembering the little device, she glanced around for the time bender. She ran her hand through the damp grass looking for it but came up empty handed.

Hot fear trickled over her. While Dane had held the device, they had both pushed the button. Hopefully, he still had the thing so they could get out of here when it reset itself.

"Dane?" she called again, this time a little louder.

A nearby groan gave her hope.

"I'm here," she said.

She could hear the splashing of water and then Dane's head popped up through the cattails. He was soaked from head to toe. Relief washed through her, though. At least he was still there with her.

"Are you all right?" She made her way over to him.

He nodded, patting himself down. "I think so. No broken bones or injuries."

"Do you still have the time bender?"

He met her gaze, his green eyes bright with concern. He got back down on his hands and knees and searched the area. With her heart in her throat, she hurried over to him, dropped to her knees next to him, and helped him search.

"I had it," he said, "when we jumped."

"I know." Her voice warbled with the fear the damn thing was lost and they'd be stuck there. Wherever there was.

He stuck his hand under the surface, disturbing the silt and turning the clear water cloudy. He froze and lifted his gaze to her. She didn't like that look at all. When he lifted his hand, it dripped mud and water. In his palm, the soiled time bender.

"Well, shit." It was the only thing she could think to say as she stared at the muddy little device.

He brushed away the mud. "The screen still works, if that's any consolation."

"Not really." Hot tears burned the backs of her eyes as she stared at the device. There was no way to know if the thing was waterproof or mud proof. "Now what?"

"I guess we wait the three days and see if it resets itself."

"And if it doesn't?" She hated asking the question, but she had to.

He said nothing as he slowly shook his head. He didn't want to voice the answer as much as she didn't want to hear it. Skye sank to the ground, not caring if she was sitting in the middle of a marshy puddle surround by cattails. A dragonfly fluttered across her vision, but she couldn't focus on it through the sudden tears that watered her eyes.

"We're never getting home, are we?" She sounded pathetic. She knew it. But she couldn't help it.

"Never is a strong word, I'd say." He used his wet tunic to further clean the device. He scraped away the mud with the edge of his tunic. "You're giving up too easily."

"I'm not giving up," she snapped. "Look at that thing, Dane. It was submerged, for God's sake. It's covered in mud. There's no way it's going to work."

"We'll just have to wait and see, won't we?"

She knew he was trying to be optimistic. He was trying to keep her from falling into a million pieces. He was trying to keep her hopeful they would, indeed, return home. But Skye wasn't so sure. She opened her mouth to reply when shouts on the other side of the river cut her off.

They both looked in the direction of the funeral procession to see they were under attack. The women ran toward the temple. Several men dressed in red and gold with leather helmets chased them down. The attackers killed the two bannermen, the drummer. One stabbed one of the women in the back. Another grabbed the second woman by the hair and yanked her back toward him. The men who had brought up the rear of the processional moved into action, fighting those who had attacked them. But not swift enough.

"The funeral procession is under attack," Skye said as she watched, horrified.

Dane rose to his full height and stuck the time bender in his pants pocket. He held a muddy hand down to her. "I think we better get out of here."

She took his hand, got to her feet. "Where are we supposed to go?"

He looked her square in the eye, a smile ticking at the corner of his mouth. "I don't know. I'm making this up as I go."

Chapter 2
Lord of the Underworld

They followed the river. With the setting sun behind them, Dane announced they were headed east. The sounds of the skirmish dwindled behind them as they made their way through the boggy ground. Skye kept close to him, thinking about nothing but the mud caked time bender and wondering if it would even work now.

"You can't give up, you know," Dane said.

She cut him a glance. "I'm not."

"You want to, though. I saw it in your face."

She hated he could read her expressions with such ease. She clenched her jaw. "We don't know if it still works. That's all. We could be stuck here."

"You don't know that. Neither do I." He stopped her with a hand on her arm. She gazed up into his clear green eyes. She always did like his eyes. "I have to believe if the screen still works, then we have a chance to get home."

She tugged the edge of her bottom lip through her teeth. "And if it doesn't—"

Before she finished, he pressed a finger against her lips and shushed her. "No more of that negative talk or worrying. Now, come on. Let's go find some place to hide out until the thing resets itself."

He took her by the hand and started walking again. He was starting to do that more and more and she was starting to like it more and more. Skye shoved her dismal thoughts of the potentially broken time bender out of her mind. As they moved along the banks of the river, the landscape changed from lush and green to dry and sandy. The temperature changed from humid to hot and arid.

In the distance on the horizon, they could see walls surrounding what was probably a city. Beyond that, a structure in the middle of construction.

Whatever it was had a large base with sides angling upward. It was not yet complete. She shaded her eyes and squinted—as if that would help.

"Do you see that?" She pointed to the structure.

"I see it," he said with a nod. "They're building something big."

"What could it be?" she wondered.

"Something to help sustain the city, maybe," he said.

She stared at the walls and then focused just behind. She could see buildings rising up and when she strained her ears, she could hear the cacophony of a thriving village. Hope sprang inside her. She glanced down at first her attire and then his. They still wore the clothes from the Citadel and, by a stroke of luck, they looked like they could belong here. She glanced up at Dane. He had several days growth of beard on his cheeks and chin giving him a rough appearance. His hair was disheveled. He had a streak of mud across his forehead.

"Are we heading to the city?" she asked.

"I think it's our only chance of survival." His gaze never left what was ahead of him and she could see the wheels turning in his head as he thought of every possible scenario once they arrived in that city. "We'll need money and food and a place to sleep."

She eyed the walls ahead and saw the open gate with carvings in the stone doors. Flanking the opening, two sentries dressed not unlike the men in the funeral procession. They each held an eight-foot spear in one hand, their feet were shoulder-width apart.

"What sort of place do you suppose this is?" she mused.

"Not sure."

The river took a turn away from the city and wound around north of the walls, disappearing in the distance. The green banks were gone, replaced by sand and red rock. The land had turned into a desert. The air had turned hot and dry. They made it to the city gate. Dane's hand tightened on hers but he didn't slow down. He didn't make eye contact with the guards, either. Skye glanced at the one on her right as they passed through the gate. The guard never even blinked as they walked by like they knew what they were doing.

Inside the walls of the city, the buildings were made of mudbrick with whitewashed walls. The place was a bustle of activity as people filled the dusty streets from one end to the other. Overhead, a canvas cover extended from the edge of one rooftop to the other doing its best to shade the street from the harsh desert sun.

Clearly, this was their central marketplace where they traded and purchased goods. On one side, there was a fruit and vegetable vendor. Next to him, the baker with a cart full of fresh baked goods. Beyond him, a vendor with dried meats hanging from his canvas-covered cart. Smelling the amalgamation of food scents made her stomach growl.

But Dane's step never faltered as he moved into the crowded street. Nor did he let go of her hand. As they walked past vendor after vendor and shop after shop, though, Skye noticed the natives had begun to notice them. So much so, they stopped and gaped openly as they passed through.

"Um, Dane?"

"I see. Just keep walking."

He'd noticed them staring, too. She focused on him, then, and saw the stiffness in his back and the tight lines across his shoulders. He was on edge. He didn't like it any more than she did.

"Has to be that flaming hair of yours," he said under his breath. "We really need to do something about that."

On instinct, she reached up and ran a hand down her tangled hair. She had always loved the color of her hair. Her father had called it the color of a shiny new penny with its bright copper strands. But maybe Dane was right. The people of the Citadel thought she was the Goddess of Fire. In wintertime, she was almost scarified to the gods because of her hair.

She would need to dye it. But how? She doubted the local store carried boxes of Nice 'N Easy.

Skye glanced around at the faces as they passed through and noticed the gathering crowed. She also noticed they were not looking at her. They were looking at *him*.

"Dane? It's not me. It's you."

"What?" He never broke his stride as he spoke.

"They're looking at you."

She watched him as he glanced around, his eyes darting from face to face. The moment he realized she was right, his jaw clenched, the muscles flexing underneath the stubble.

"Hell," he muttered.

"Now what?"

"We get out of this city."

Still holding onto her, he spun around and started back the way they had come heading right for the open gate. The crowd parted making way for them. Skye kept her gaze on the open gate, her heart suddenly ramming hard in her chest. She didn't like the staring.

A shout rose up near the gate. She could see a commotion there. Several people ran inside. The two guards on the outside slammed the gate shut, sliding a bar in place to seal everyone inside. Skye and Dane halted.

The crowd turned away from them and looked toward the closed gate and the new arrivals. Skye recognized them immediately as several who were part of the funeral procession. Two women, one with a bloody nose and torn gown. The woman who wore black and had jewels in her hair looked as though she had been beaten. Her face was dirty and tear-streaked. Only two of the men remained. They looked as though they had barely survived the attack.

"Those people," she said, but halted.

"Right," Dane said, understanding what she meant to say without having to say it. "They were attacked."

The woman with the jewels spotted them then. Her dark eyes widened. She took slow steps toward them, pausing in front of Dane and then dropping to her knees, bowing her head low to the ground. All those around them followed her example and dropped to the ground, bowing.

"What the…" But Skye never finished.

"Well, this is different," he muttered.

"Looks like it's your turn to be worshipped." She smirked, almost laughing at the idea of Dane being worshipped as she had in the Citadel.

"What do I do?" he asked.

"Tell them to rise."

He cleared his throat. "Arise, friends."

"Arise?" she repeated.

The woman stood first. She bowed her head again, keeping her eyes down. "Your lordship."

"Your lordship?" Skye blurted without thinking.

One of the soldiers at the woman's side glared at Skye. She didn't like that look at all.

"You dare disrespect the Lord of the Underworld?" The woman spat at Skye.

Skye choked back a laugh. "Lord of the Underworld?"

"A god among all those who stand in his presence. I am not worthy, your lordship."

"What's your name?" Dane asked the girl.

"I am Amatta, princess and daughter of Pharaoh Ra-Sha-Tor."

Dane shifted from one foot to the other, clearly uncomfortable with the proclamation he was a god. Skye couldn't help it. She snickered.

"Now you get to see what it's like," she whispered.

"You come on the day I lay to rest my beloved husband, Prince Nefer-Amun." At last she lifted her head, her dark eyes wide and full of wonder. "You can resurrect him."

"Uh, no, I cannot."

"You can," she insisted. "You are the Lord of the Underworld, God of the Undead." She reached for his hand. "You must come with me at once to the Temple of the Dead and bring him back from the Astral Kingdom before it's too late."

"My princess, it is not safe. The Omoth may still be out there," the soldier said.

"The Omoth? Who or what is that?" Dane asked.

Nope. Skye really didn't like were this was going.

"We have been at war with the Omoth for nearly an age. They wish to conquer us. They killed my love," Amatta said. She pulled him toward her. "Please, come. Come save my prince."

Dane glanced back at Skye with question on his face, looking for help. She shrugged. What was she supposed to do? She couldn't help him. When he realized she had nothing, he gently tugged his hand from the girl's.

"I can assure you, princess, I have no power to resurrect your prince. I'm just a man. Not a god."

"Please, I beg you." Tears filled her round eyes. She clasped her hands together in front of her.

"We will take you to the tomb," one of the guards said, stepping up. "We will make sure you're protected from the Omoth."

With a sigh, Dane finally nodded. "All right. I'll come."

Before they could take a step toward the gate, the princess pointed at Skye. "Not her. She is a sorceress."

"What? No, I'm not," Skye said, shaking her head.

"I assure you she is no sorceress," Dane said. "She has no power."

But the girl shook her head. "My guardsmen will take her away from here. She cannot come with us to the sacred temple. Her evil magic will destroy all and turn the dead against us."

Two guards flanked Skye then, one taking her by the arm. Panic set in. "Dane—"

"She comes with me," Dane said, his tone firm and unyielding. "Or I don't go at all."

Amatta glared at Skye before she finally glanced back at Dane. "I cannot defy your wishes, your lordship. She may come but she will remain outside the temple with my guardsmen."

"Fine. Let's go." He waved toward the gate.

Dane, the princess, and a few others headed toward the gate. Before Skye could take a step, one of the guards bound her wrists together with rope.

"Is that really necessary?" she asked.

But they ignored her. One gave her a shove toward the gate. Both of them fell in step beside her as they escorted her through the gate behind Dane and the princess.

Skye knew, in that instance, she hated it here.

Chapter 3
The Omoth

Dane resisted the urge to look back to make sure Skye was okay. Knowing she was behind him, even if she was guarded, gave him comfort. The princess walked beside him, keeping pace with him which was impressive since he was a head taller than her.

It didn't escape his notice the girl looked like she'd been beaten. Nor did it escape his notice the other woman looked as though she had been attacked. Her nose was bloody and her gown was torn. His first instinct was to find whoever had done that to her and kill them.

But he reined that in for Skye's sake. He didn't want to go with the princess any more than Skye wanted him to. And calling him the Lord of the Underworld? That was crazy talk. Now he understood how Skye felt when she was branded Goddess of Fire. She hadn't been too keen on it, either.

The two guards, Skye, Dane, the princess and her remaining lady all exited the gate and headed back to the east. In the distance, he could see the river as it cut its way through the desert. The rocky, sandy landscape turned from brown to green and lush and verdant. He knew they were headed right for the temple he and Skye had seen when they first arrived.

He didn't want to admit he thought the time bender was busted. Finding it submerged and caked in mud didn't bode well. He doubted it would work again. But he didn't want Skye to know that. He didn't need her frantic. He needed her calm and to have faith.

No matter what happened, though, he made a silent vow to take care of her and make sure she was okay. Sure, he'd promised William Ransom he would protect her but now he was doing it because he wanted to, not because he was hired to.

"The temple is ahead." The princess motioned to the mountain.

"Perhaps, princess, we should return to the city and wait until morning," he suggested. Then he could figure out a way to get away from her and get them both out of there.

Her lady-in-waiting gave a glance between him and the princess and looked as though she was ready to agree with him.

But it was not to be. Amatta shook her head. "No. It must be tonight. It has already been two sunsets since my love died. If you are to return him to the living, we cannot wait another sunset."

Dane suppressed the groan that wanted to escape. How could he tell her he wasn't equipped with the kind of magic she wanted him to do? He was nothing more than a mortal man with no powers whatsoever. He couldn't resurrect anyone.

As the sun dipped closer to the horizon, the wind cooled off the hot desert sand. There was a definite chill in the air. They made their way to the tomb. Once they reached it, Skye and the two guards waited outside while the princess led him into the shadowy darkness. Her lady-in-waiting followed them inside but paused at the mouth of the tomb.

Inside, a stone sarcophagus sat under one flickering torch. Intricate carved shapes reminding him of hieroglyphics were along the sides and top. The princess motioned toward the tomb, an expectant look on her face.

Dane paused at the edge of the sarcophagus, wondering what she expected him to do. He pretended to examine the top, looking for a way to push open the lid.

"You need to see his body, don't you?" The princess said, then shouted, "Guards!"

The two guarding Skye entered the tomb. He peered at the darkened opening, resisting the urge to bolt for it, grab Skye, and make a run for it.

The men pushed aside the lid with a violent shove. It landed with a crash on the floor, cracking. The princess frowned at the men and motioned for them to get out. They scurried by her and exited.

"It makes no matter," she said mentioning to the broken lid of the sarcophagus. "He will rise and walk the land again."

Dane peered down at the mummy-wrapped body. The arms were folded across the chest, the legs were bound tightly together. Nothing of the person inside was visible to him. Surrounding the body, were several clay jars in various sizes. Curious, he reached for one of the lids. Inside, a human heart. He released the lid so suddenly it clattered against the jar.

He remembered, somewhere in the deep recesses of his mind, the ancient Egyptians removed all the organs from the dead and buried them with the body.

"What are you waiting for?" Impatience laced her tone as she shifted from one foot to the other.

He met her dark glittering gaze. Her kohl-lined eyes were sparkled with unshed tears. "Why do you not raise him from the dead?"

"You must understand, princess—"

"*Dane!*"

The shriek from Skye outside the tomb made him bolt into a run. He ignored the princess as he rushed past her. She called out to him, but he ignored her as he made for the exit and ran by her lady-in-waiting. As soon as he exited, he halted.

The two guards were dead, lying in pool of blood. Arrows stuck out of both their necks. A man wearing a helm with a red plume held a knife to Skye's throat. Four men stood behind them, all armed with short swords and crossbows. They were the same men who had attacked the funeral procession earlier. He heard an intake of breath next to him and knew the princess had arrived.

"Let her go," Dane said.

He had no weapon. Nothing he could use to fight the men. Nothing but his hands and his wits.

But the man with the plumed helm was not interested in talking to him. His gaze pinpointed the princess. "It's the princess we want."

"You will not have me, Caius," she said, her tone snooty.

"Then the girl dies." He pressed the knife into Skye's throat, drawing blood.

"No," Dane said.

Caius' gaze flickered to him, then. "And who are you?"

Before he could answer, the princess said, "He is the Lord of the Underworld. He will kill you with his god-magic."

Well, crap. How was he supposed to kill this guy with god-magic he didn't have?

Caius eyed him warily, his knife hand going slack. He looked as though he considered letting her go, but then something flickered across his eyes and he tightened his grip again on Skye.

"The Omoth do not believe in your gods, princess."

"The Omoth only believe in annihilation," she retorted.

An explosion rocked the ground with such a violent vibration, they all stumbled. Caius dropped his hand from her neck enough to give her the leverage she needed to shove out of Caius' grasp. She fell toward Dane. He caught her in his arms, pulled her into a protective embrace. Caius had lost interest in her and now turned to eye the plume of fire and smoke rising in the distance where the village had once been.

"NO!" the princess shrieked. She started to run toward it, but Dane caught her by the arm.

"It's no use," he said.

Caius flashed her a wicked smile. "Our fight with you is not over yet, *princess.*"

He and his men left them there at the mouth of the tomb.

Chapter 4
Sorceress

As soon as he was out of ear shot, the princess reeled on Skye. Fury lined her face. Her fists were clenched. "This is your doing."

Surprise flickered through Skye as she looked at the woman, her cheeks red with her anger. "I had nothing to do with this."

The princess took a threatening step toward her. "If it hadn't been for your...*sorcery*, none of this would have happened."

Dane stepped between them. He gave Skye a nudge behind him. "None of this was her fault, princess. She has no sorcery. She's mortal, like me."

Skye peered around Dane to see Amatta's angry gaze flicker up to his face. Slowly, her fingers uncurled. She lifted her shoulders and straightened her back.

"I do not believe, your lordship, that she had nothing to do with this. We escaped the Omoth when we made it to the village. And yet they return to attack." She waved toward the flames in the distance. "And now the village has been destroyed. Yet you tell me she is not to be blamed."

"I am not." Skye pressed her lips together, her own anger surging forward. How dare this princess accuse her of destroying the village. And was she insinuating she had something to do with the attack on them outside the tomb? The girl was clearly not in her right mind.

"Your highness," this from her female companion who had remained behind the princess and silent until now. She placed a hand on the princess's arm. "You are fatigued. It has been a trying day. Let us reconvene at the palace and discuss later."

All the fight seemed to go out of Amatta. She inhaled a slow breath, then exhaled it just as slowly. "You're right, Gaia." She turned to Dane then. "You will return with us to the palace. My father will want to know you." And then her gaze landed on Skye. "As for *her*..." She paused, a look of distaste on her face. "She may come as well."

"Gee, thanks," Skye muttered.

She certainly didn't feel any love from Princess Amatta, though.

They walked for what seemed like hours under the silvery full moon across the desert past the village. Embers smoldered still along the crumbled walls. The princess paused to look on, sadness creasing her face. Her lady put a hand on her arm and urged her to come away. They continued on their way. As they passed by, they could see a few people inside trying to put out the remaining fires and salvage what was left of the village.

"Is there nothing we can do?" Skye whispered to Dane.

He merely shook his head.

She supposed he was right. Here they were. Strangers in a strange land once again. It was a situation they found themselves in all too often these days.

More walking. They put distance between them and the burning village. Ahead, they could see a line of torches in iron brackets flickering on the night breeze leading up to the palace. The ground turned from dirt to smooth pave stone the closer they got to the palace. It was a large, rectangular temple-like structure with a central roof higher than that of the sides.

The door to the entrance was painted a dark red. Guards flanked the door and lined the front. As they entered, they gave them a sidelong glance that did not escape Skye's notice. This felt much like arriving at the Citadel, except on a much grander scale. And here, she was not considered a goddess.

They entered what appeared to be the main hall. The cream-colored tile floor was polished to a high shine. Gigantic columns lined the main hall, giving it a grand appearance. As they entered, they were greeted by an older man with silver hair and black eyes. He wore a flowing black robe trimmed in red and gold and sandals on his feet. A gold circlet wrapped around his forehead. Gaudy rings adorned nearly every finger. He hurried toward Amatta.

"What kept you? Your king has been asking for you all evening. We heard about the village and—" He noticed Skye and Dane then. His gaze flicked over Dane but paused on Skye. His eyes went wide and round as he took a step back and put his hand up as if to ward her off. "Sorceress!"

Skye rolled her eyes. Dane positioned himself between her and the newcomer. "She isn't."

Amatta moved to stand by the man's side, making it seem as though she'd picked a side. "He claims that, but we were attacked at the tomb. I believe it is her fault."

Skye huffed out breath. "For the last time, I had nothing to do with that."

The man snapped his fingers twice. Two guards arrived, as though melting out of the shadows. They wore black leather armor with silver studs, a helm that nearly covered their faces, and carried a six-foot long spear. Skye glanced around, then, and saw them positioned between each pillar. With their black leather armor, they appeared to blend in very well with the shadows and appeared almost invisible.

"Take her away."

The two guards each took her by one of her arms. She immediately struggled against them. "Let me go. Dane, don't let them take me."

Panic flickered through his eyes. As he took a step toward Skye, the newcomer put a hand up to stop him.

"You will not interfere," he said.

Dane glanced at the princess, a pleading expression on his face. But she ignored him. She had a smug smile on her lips as the guards dragged her away. It was clear to Skye in that moment, the princess truly thought she was a sorceress and that she had everything to do with the attack at the tomb.

She struggled between the two men as they dragged her away. Yet again, she was separated from Dane. Yet again, he had the time bender on his person. Yet again, they would be forced to wait out the time bender resetting in another horrible place.

We stick together. No matter what.

His words echoed back at her. So much for that. They couldn't seem to stick together even if they wanted. Somehow, they always ended up separated. When would they learn to stay out of sight of the strangers they encountered in the new worlds in which they landed?

She let the fight go out of her as they rounded a corner out of sight of Dane and the others. There wasn't anything Dane could do to convince the princess she had nothing to do with what happened at the tomb. The princess had convinced herself she had some kind of magic and made it all happen.

Skye resigned herself to being taken away by the guards. They headed down a long hallway and exited the palace from a side door, entering a moonlit courtyard. She could see nothing but shapes in the darkness. Statues, palm trees, other plants. In the distance, several buildings that looked like temples. They headed down a path paved with stone that glistened in the moonlight. Ahead, she could see an iron gate.

She knew that's where they were headed. She didn't even try to argue. They went through the gate, down a dusty path toward a cluster of one-story buildings. Torchlight flickered here and there and as they neared. She could see the torches in the ground flanking an entrance to the building. One of the guards shoved open the door and pushed her inside.

"Wait here," the first one said, more to the second than to her.

She shifted her weight on her feet as she watched him walk down a long hallway to the door at the end. He pounded on the door. Someone opened it. They spoke in low tones. The door slammed. The guard stepped back, waiting. A few minutes later, the door came open again. A barefoot man wearing a long dingy white linen robe with a frayed hem fell in step beside the guard and approached.

The man had a face like a roadmap, aged by wind and sun. His bronze skin was a stark contrast next to the dingy robe. He looked her over with a critical eye. It did not escape Skye's notice his gaze paused for a long moment on her red hair.

"Come with me, girl."

The guards released her, turned and left. The door behind her slammed shut with a finality she didn't like. The man waved her to follow as he took off down the long hallway. At the end, across from the room he'd exited, he pushed open the door and gave her a shove inside. Without another word, he slammed the door shut and locked her inside.

Skye stood there staring at the door, tempted to pound on it and beg to be let out. But she knew it wouldn't do any good. She fought the hot tears of frustration and rage. She would not cry.

"Hello?"

The soft female voice behind her made her spin around, her heart a jackhammer in her chest. The girl sat on a narrow bed on one side of the room, her knees drawn up to her chest.

"Hello," Skye said, finally finding her voice.

"Do you want to sit?" The girl waved to the empty bed across from her.

Skye took a moment to examine the room. It was small, had one small window with bars on it. The two narrow beds were shoved against each wall, a small rickety table between them with a candle burning in a holder. Nothing more. She took a tentative step toward the other bed and slowly lowered to the edge. The mattress felt like straw and was covered with a tattered blanket that had definitely seen better days.

"My name is Malika. What's yours?"

She considered. In the last few time jumps, her name had always given people pause. For the sake of simplicity, she decided she would honor her dead mother.

"Emily."

The girl smiled at her. It was a sad smile that didn't reach her baleful eyes. "That's a pretty name."

"So is Malika," Skye said.

"We should get some sleep," she suggested. "The come before dawn."

"Who does?"

"The slave lords." With a yawn, the girl rolled to her side. "Good night."

But Skye knew she would never sleep with the thought of slave lords hanging over her head.

Chapter 5
To the Quarry

Dane watched them drag Skye away, his heart beating at a rapid pace. His gut twisted in a sickly knot. How many times was this going to happen to them? How many times would they endure being separated in the crazy time jumps? Angry, he reeled on Amatta. He wanted to wipe her smug smile off her face.

"Where are they taking her?"

"To the slave quarters," the man answered.

"Slave quarters?" Dane repeated. Oh, shit. How the hell was he supposed to get her out of that?

"You cannot tell me she had nothing to do with what happened at the tomb." The princess folded her arms over her chest, looking defiant. "Or the village."

"She destroyed the village?" the man asked. Anger creased his forehead.

"She didn't. She had nothing to do with any of it." Dane gritted out the words through his clenched teeth. He raked his hand through his hair, frustration edging through him.

At least he still had the device tucked in his pocket. It was safe, for the moment. With any luck, it would reset itself and they would get closer to home with the next time jump.

"Princess, who is this man?" the newcomer asked, still eyeing Dane.

"Do you not know, Zephrym?" She didn't hide the incredulity in her voice.

Zephrym gave him a sideways glance. His eye narrowed as he looked, really looked, at Dane. Surprise came over his face. He clutched his chest as he stepped back, shaking his head.

"It cannot be," he whispered.

"It is. He is the Lord of the Underworld," Amatta said.

"Your lordship." Zephrym fell to his knees, his head bowed low.

Dane resisted the sigh of annoyance that wanted to erupt. "Get up, Zephrym. You don't need to bow to me."

"You are a *god* among men." His head dropped to his chest, his voice was muffled.

"Stand up." Dane reached for him and pulled him to his feet. The last thing he needed was for people to start falling to their knees and bowing to him.

The princess beamed. "In the morning, the Pharaoh will want to meet you."

She had clearly forgotten all about her dead lover he was to resurrect.

"The Pharaoh?"

What kind of world was this? Ancient Egypt? It didn't seem like it, but then, he supposed anything was possible. The few places they'd landed weren't exactly what they seemed. And the time bender, he knew, was faulty. The last time jump had led them to a place that wasn't exactly in history. He started to think the thing was bending time in new, strange ways. Where they would end up next was anyone's guess.

She gave an emphatic nod. "Zephrym, will you show his grace to his sleeping quarters?" She turned to him, then, gave him a quick bow of the head. "Tomorrow, we will find you better arrangements befitting that of a god."

Dane suppressed an inward groan. He really wished they would stop calling him a god. Now, he truly understood how Skye felt with the citizens of the Citadel calling her a goddess. It was unnerving.

"Come." He waved for Dane to follow him. "You will want rest and food and…" He looked him up and down. "Perhaps new clothes. As for you, princess—"

"I will go to my king father at once." She gave a low bow to Dane, then headed off with her lady through the palace.

Zephrym waved for him to follow. Dane glanced down at clothes and saw they were mud-stained and dirty. He fell in step behind him.

Zephrym said nothing has he took him through a maze of corridors in the palace. This was much more complex than the Citadel. He doubted he would ever find his way out and back to Skye.

The man paused at a door, opened it, and waved him inside. Dane stepped into the room, but Zephrym didn't follow. He stood in the open doorway, gave a low bow of his head.

"I bid you goodnight."

With that, he shut the door and left Dane alone.

The room was plain. With only a bed and one window. A candle burned in a holder on the table next to the bed. He sat on the edge of it, expelling a heated breath. He wasn't sure how he and Skye would find each other again. But as he sat there, he vowed he would get back to her no matter what it took.

~ ⧗ ~

Morning came far too quickly. Skye hadn't slept at all. She jumped to her feet when she heard the door rattle and then open a moment later. Malika was on her feet in seconds, too, smoothing her hand down her black hair. Morning light streamed in through the one window, leaving slats of sunlight on the floor.

The man from last night stepped inside. He first looked at Malika.

"Why are you not at work?"

"N-no one came to wake me, my lord."

He scowled. "Go. Two lashes for being late." She dropped her head and hurried out of the room. The man turned to Skye then. "As for you, come with me." He turned toward the open door.

"Where are you taking me?"

He paused, gave her a glare over his shoulder. "Do not question me, girl."

"I have a name."

"I don't care what your name is. I'll call you girl or bitch or whatever I want." He reached for her then, wrapped his hand around her upper arm. His fingers dug into the fleshy part of her arm. "You will come and you will keep your mouth shut."

Skye had no choice but to obey him. She followed him out of the tiny room. Instead of heading toward the front where she had entered the night before, he took her through the building to another exit. They stepped outside in the morning light. And there was Malika. A guard had just finished whipping her back.

Horror rippled through Skye as she watched the girl, who couldn't be any older than Tia, hurry past the guards and through a gate in the mud-brick wall surrounding the dusty yard. Her face somehow remained impassive as she exited. In the distance, Skye could hear shouts, the clang of tools and other construction noise. Over the edge of the wall, she could see the half-built building.

The man led Skye to the center of the yard where Malika had been moments before.

"Two lashes," he said to one of the guards.

Before Skye realized what was happening, the guard with the whip swung the weapon in a wide arc. It slammed into her back. The force of it, the agony of it, made her fall to her knees. She cried out as the pain seared through her. She didn't have time to recover from the first lash when the second one ripped through her. Crying out, she fell face first into the ground. Dirt stuck to her damp cheeks.

"Get her up. Take her out there," said the man.

Rough hands grabbed her by the arms and dragged her to her feet. The horrible pain was so excruciating, a wave of nausea cascaded through her. Dizziness swept through her. She thought she might vomit, yet she had nothing to eat or drink since she couldn't remember when.

The guards dragged her out the gate and into the searing morning heat. Were they taking her out to work as slave labor? As they neared the edge of the construction site, they paused. The men spoke to someone who appeared to be in charge. They slapped iron manacles on her wrists with enough chain to give her a small range of movement.

"Take her to the quarry."

Sweat beaded her forehead. Pain lanced through her with every step. And all she could think about was getting out of this hell hole and back to Dane, back *home*. Tears clouded her vision but she knew crying now would do her no good. She would have to suck it up. She'd have to find a way to survive this until she could make a break for it.

The manacles on her wrists would definitely impede her, but she would find a way. As God was her witness, she would find a way.

Chapter 6
Chaos and Balance

Dane hadn't slept. He'd laid on the bed staring up at the ceiling wondering where Skye was and if she was okay. He had let her down by not being able to stick with her.

No matter what. That's what he'd promised her. And here he was in a room in the palace while she was…hell, he didn't even know where she was. He had to find her. The more time that passed, the more he worried for her safety. He didn't like seeing the guards drag her off.

A swift knock on his door preceded it's opening. He quickly got to his feet as Zephrym entered carrying an armload of clothes. Behind him, another person who appeared to be a servant carrying a large animal head that looked eerily like an Anubis.

"I have come to escort you to the bathing chamber. Then you will dress." Zephrym dumped the clothes on the bed. The other servant placed the Anubis head next to the clothes, and hurried away as though his feet were on fire.

Dane picked up the Anubis and discovered it was nothing more than an elaborate headdress. Eye and nose holes were cut out and suddenly he realized they expected him to wear *that.*

"No." He dropped the Anubis back to the bed.

"You must. You, as Lord of the Underworld, may not look upon the Pharaoh and his wife with your own eyes."

"Why not?"

"It is forbidden. This is known." He waved him toward the door. "Come. The bathing chamber is ready for you."

Reluctantly, Dane followed him from his room.

"The bathing chamber sits atop a natural spring. I think you'll find it to be the perfect temperature for you," the man gushed as they walked.

Dane resisted the urge to roll his eyes. He didn't particularly care if the water had the perfect temperature or not. All he really cared about was getting the hell out of there.

The bathing chamber was only a few steps away. The bathtub—if it could be called that—looked like a large in-ground pool with terra cotta tiles. Steam rose off the surface. There, several attendees waited to assist him. Several *female* attendees.

Zephrym clapped his hands twice and two of the girls hurried over. Dane put a hand up to stop them.

"I don't need help. Send them away."

"But, your lordship—"

"I said send them away," he repeated. "All of them."

"It's simply not done," Zephrym argued, shaking his head.

"It is now."

Dane stood his ground, glaring at the older man. He refused to back down. He didn't need young, female girls fawning all over him. Of course, any other man would have welcomed that but Dane was in no mood to entertain the ladies. He could almost hear his friend, Nick Slaughter, berating him for his decision.

He hadn't even thought about Nick since he started all the time traveling business with Skye. But now, as he watched Zephrym shoo the girls out of the room, he wondered what had become of him and the protection agency.

Glancing around the room to make sure he was alone, he disrobed and slipped into the steaming water. Much to his annoyance, Zephrym was right in that the water temperature *was* fairly perfect. He dunked his head under the water. When he came back up, he was startled to see a woman standing on the other side of the pool.

Her glossy black hair hung over one shoulder in a long cascading wave. She wore a black gown that hugged each and every curve of her thin body. The long sleeves ended in a point on each hand at her middle finger. Her full lips were painted bright red.

"You must be the infamous Lord of the Underworld everyone is whispering about." One corner of her bright red mouth lifted in a half-cocked grin.

He stilled, watching her as she took carful steps around the edge of the pool, getting closer to him.

"Who are you?"

"Oh, fear not, *your lordship*." Sarcasm laced the words *your lordship*. "I don't intend to hurt you, if that's what you're worried about." She paused at the edge of the pool, standing over his head.

"What do you want?" He tried to use his best authoritative voice, but it was difficult when he was naked and in unfamiliar surroundings.

"I think you and I both know you are not really the Lord of the Underworld, don't we?" She dropped to her knees and braced her hands on the edge of the pool. She leaned close. "You asked who I was but I think the real question is…*who are you?*"

A prickling sensation crawled up the back of his neck, tingling at the base of his skull under his damp hair. How did she know? As he contemplated how to respond to her, she continued.

"These sad people will do anything to restore order to their little kingdom. Even brand a mere mortal a god who happens to bear a remarkable resemblance to the Lord of the Underworld." She heaved a sighed. "It's pathetic, really. They have no understanding of the Omoth or what they truly want."

"And you do?"

She snickered. "Of course, I do."

While he was insanely curious about the Omoth and what they truly wanted, he decided to answer her question first. "You're right. I'm a mere mortal. I tried to convince Amatta otherwise, but she wouldn't accept it. She thought I could resurrect her lover."

The woman rolled her eyes. "Such a simpleton, the princess. The prince is dead and will remain so. There is no coming back for him since all of his organs have been removed."

Her comment gave him pause and he wondered. If the prince still had all his organs, could he be resurrected?

Her gaze came back to him as she looked him over with an appreciative grin. It appeared she liked what she saw. "I'm glad to know my instincts weren't wrong about you. I've been watching you since you arrived."

Did she mean arrived at the place or arrived in this time? He resisted the urge to glance at his pants where the time bender still resided in his pocket.

"That's nice." He shifted his weight in the pool, a little uncomfortable at the thought of this woman spying on him. "You know who I am. Now, are you going to tell me who you are?"

Her smile was genuine, bright, and lit up her eyes with life. She rose to her full height. "Unlike you, I *am* a goddess. I bring balance to chaos. Harmony to discord. Order to disorder. I am called Raza and I am here to help you."

He almost snorted. "Help me? How, exactly?"

"These pitiful fools who have claimed you as their Lord of the Underworld will, at some point, expect you to perform miracles. They truly believe you are here to help them defeat the Omoth."

"But I'm not," Dane pointed out.

"No. This is merely a stop on your journey."

Something about the way she said it gave him that tingling sensation again. As if she knew more about him than she was letting on. If she truly was a goddess, then perhaps she did.

"In truth, I'm here to help them defeat the Omoth. Not you. But since they have selected you as their champion, then there is no need to make myself visible to them. It will only confuse their poor little minds." She glanced over her cuticles, as if she were bored by her own conversation.

"Okay. I'll play. How, exactly, are you to help them defeat the Omoth?"

"Why, by using you, of course."

"And how is that going to work?"

Again, that cocky grin with one corner of her mouth appeared. "You'll have to wait and see, won't you? And I've kept you quite long enough. The little man with the squint will be back soon to hurry you along. You will do everything they say and I…" She paused, grinned, looking pleased with herself. "I will be there to assist. For now, farewell."

And then she was gone in a puff of black and gray smoke.

Chapter 7
The Slave Pit

It had been one of the strangest interactions Dane had ever had. If he hadn't seen Raza disappear, he would have never believed it. He had no idea what she meant by assisting him, either. But as she left him, he thought of Skye and wondered if there was a way he could get Raza's help getting back to her.

After washing his hair and body, he hoisted out of the pool, drying off with the towels the servant girls left behind. As he wrapped it around his waist, Zephrym reappeared as if he had been waiting for him to finish.

"Ah, good. Now let's get you dressed."

Dane scooped up his discarded clothes and followed the old man from the bathing chamber. As he walked, he fumbled with his pants pocket until his fingers landed on the time bender. He clutched it in his palm, relieved to have the little device in his hand.

Back in his room, Zephrym motioned toward the clothes on the bed. "You must be quick. Pharaoh and his Great Royal Wife will be waiting to meet you."

He shoved material at Dane and motioned toward the privacy screen on the other side of the room. Still clutching the device, he moved behind the screen and dumped the clothes on the floor. He took a minute to examine the device to see if it still worked. As far as he could tell, the screen on the device was still working and lit. But that didn't mean it would reset itself and they would be able to time jump again.

He glanced around, looking for a place to stash the device but there wasn't any. And, really, did he want to leave the little device behind where it could be found and confiscated?

He clutched it in his fist again, trying to decide what to do with it. For the moment, he put it on the floor between his bare feet.

The clothes he'd been given were less than satisfactory. In fact, they were downright wrong for him. The bottom was a wrap that tightened around his waist and tucked into the front. There was no shirt or tunic.

"There's no tunic," Dane said.

"You will wear something befitting a god," Zephrym replied.

Dane peered around the edge of the privacy screen. The man held up two gold armbands.

Great.

He picked up the time bender, still trying to figure out what to do with the damn thing. He tucked it in the folds of the material of his wrap. Then stepped out from behind the screen. Zephrym insisted on the gold armbands. Reluctantly, Dane slipped on first one and then the other. Then the old man held up a large colorful collar necklace. He didn't give Dane any time to refuse before he was putting it around his neck and fastening it.

"And these." Zephrym nodded to the sandals on the floor by the side of the bed.

Dane glanced around looking for his shoes from the Citadel but they were nowhere in sight.

"I'm not wearing those." He pointed to the sandals.

"Why not?"

"Because they're *sandals.*"

He glared at Zephrym and then down at the horrible sandals. He had often told his colleague, Nick, that if he was found wearing any type of open-toed shoe it was definitely time for an intervention.

"If you're looking for your other shoes, they were taken away."

With a frown, Dane had no choice but to put on the damn shoes. He was just thankful Nick wasn't around to make fun of him about it.

The final humiliation was that of the Anubis mask. Pulling it over his head, the inside smelled like death and plastic. His stomach clenched, threatening to heave. And he couldn't breathe in deep and exhale because of the disgusting stench. He could barely see out of the tiny eye holes. To make matters worse, the thing was heavy. Already his head started to throb from the immense weight of the Anubis. To compensate, his muscles tightened. He knew, before all of this was over, his would have a sore neck, shoulders, and back.

"Now we are ready," Zephrym said with a confident nod. "We go to meet the Pharaoh and his Great Royal Wife."

Dane was *not* looking forward to it.

~ ⧗ ~

Someone shoved a copper chisel into Skye's hand and ordered her to work. But she was still in too much pain to do much more than remain perfectly still. She sat in a limp heap, her hands in her lap. Her mouth was dry. The heat was unbearable. All she wanted to do was get out of there. Even if that meant time jumping again.

"You best get to work, girl."

She ignored the person—a woman—who had been trying to get her attention for the last several minutes. She didn't want anything to do with anyone here.

"Girl."

She was aware the woman had been watching her since the guards dumped her in the quarry. She was aware the woman had been trying to get her to work. She clutched the chisel tight. Her hand sweated around the handle. The skin on her back tightened where she'd been lashed. She could feel the ooze of blood trickling down her back.

She replayed the moment over and over in her head. She wished she hadn't been such a wimp about it. She should have been stronger. Taken it. Not allowed them to make her fall to her knees and cry out. She *needed* to be stronger.

But she wasn't.

She wasn't like Malika. She took her lashes and went on about her day.

Nor was she like Tia. She'd taken it. The girl *accepted* it as though it was normal.

Now Skye recalled the horror of seeing the blood clotting along the lashes on Tia's back. How she had worried for her and immediately wanted to get her to a healer. How the girl shrugged it off as if it were nothing.

Skye was nothing more than a weakling. She depended on Dane for everything since their time jumping began. He'd been there for her in Scotland when Robert the Bruce wanted to marry her off. He'd been there for her when Sovold had tried to marry her and then sacrifice her. He'd even been there for her when Ridgewood had tried to take her from the Citadel.

And what had she done for him? What had she done to keep from falling into the hands of the enemy? Nothing. That's what. She was a failure. A weak stupid girl. Maybe she deserved to die here.

The woman who had been trying to get her attention moved closer, her chains clinking. "I said, *girl*."

"I heard you the first time and every time since. Now go away and let me be," Skye snapped.

The vehemence in her voice surprised even her. When the woman flinched, guilt flickered through her. Even so, she didn't shrink away.

"If you don't put that chisel to use, then you will suffer more punishment," the old woman said. "This is known."

Skye finally turned her head and looked at her. Her face was bronzed by wind and sun. There were several crinkles around her eyes, her mouth, and lining her cheeks. But there was a bright light in her blue eyes. Her long salt and pepper hair was loose. A few strands blew across her face. She didn't even try to move them out of the way. She sat there, staring at her with condemnation and a hint of worry.

"Why do you care?" Skye asked.

"Bah." She spat on the ground. "Maybe I shouldn't. Maybe you're not worth it. But I've seen the way they treat those who don't work." She glanced out to the quarry, as if saying the words aloud would bring the slave lords' scrutiny. "They have killed workers for not working. Beat them to death right here in the middle of the quarry while everyone looked on. Do you want to end up like that?"

Skye looked down at the chisel in her hand. Her fingers tightened around the handle. "No."

Because she really didn't want to die in his horrid place. Alone.

"Then you best work. I will show you."

She had her own copper chisel in her hand. Manacles were on her wrists like Skye but she managed to get to her feet and motion for her to do the same. It took some effort. The pain from the lashes seared through her as she stood. It took all her strength to ignore it and follow the woman through the quarry to the rockface where several workers were hard at work.

"Like this."

She started chipping away at the stone and eventually cut away a large brick-size piece. As she pulled it away and dropped it in a nearby basket, Skye saw the woman's fingers were raw, red, bleeding. Her nails were nothing but nubs. And a pang of pity and then guilt went through her.

Here she was wallowing in her own pain over the two lashes on her back when this woman had been chiseling away at the stone for…well, she had no idea how long.

Clutching her chisel, she began to chip away at the rock. As she did, she realized it was limestone.

The Ancient Egyptians used limestone to construct their pyramids and their buildings. It occurred to her, then, the building under construction she and Dane saw…the one with the slanted walls…must be a pyramid. And these workers were helping build it.

Slaves.

Men. Women.

And, oh God, even children.

As she continued to half-heartedly chip away, she glanced around the quarry. Yes, children. They were chained and tasked with picking up the full baskets of limestone and depositing them into a larger bucket which was then hauled away. Probably to the construction site.

"You're doing great," the woman encouraged.

"What is your name?" Skye asked.

"Hepsheba."

"It's nice to meet you, Hepsheba," Skye said. "I'm Emily."

They chiseled away in silence for a long moment. Then, the woman said, "They brought you today, didn't they?"

"Yes," Skye said.

"From the mountain?"

Her brows knit. "I don't understand."

Hepsheba glanced behind her to make sure no slave lords were within earshot. Even so, she lowered her voice. "They raid the mountain villages and bring the women and children and weak men here. The young men are to be trained and put into service in Pharaoh's legion." She paused again, swallowed hard. Tears watered her eyes. "And then burn down the villages."

Bastards.

Fury boiled through her as she punched the stone with the tip if the chisel. The small brick-size piece came free of the wall and tumbled to the ground in front of her. Without missing a beat, Hepsheba picked it up and tossed it in the basket with hers.

"You lived in one of those villages, didn't you?" Skye asked.

"They took us. Separated me from my family. They killed my husband and took my son-in-law. I haven't seen my daughter and granddaughter since." She glanced around the quarry, as if she could spot her missing family among the sunburned, sweat-lined faces.

Skye bit her bottom lip to keep from swearing the words that wanted to erupt. It would do no good here. She thought of the injustice that had been done to the innocent people, the terror they must have gone through. Working in the quarry was no place for his old woman. Or any of them for that matter.

And she didn't know how she was going to do it, but as she chiseled another brick from the stone, she had decided then and there she would free the slaves.

All of them.

Chapter 8
The Pharaoh and the God

The walk to the throne room seemed an eternity with the ghastly, stinking mask covering his face, pressing down on his head and shoulders. It was hard to breathe and even harder to see. Dane kept looking down at his feet so he could see where he was going.

"You must keep your head up," Zephrym ordered. "Look his royal majesty in the eye."

"You said I couldn't look at him," Dane said, his voice muffled.

"I said you couldn't look at him with your own eyes. You will be looking through the mask as Lord of the Underworld."

Dane nearly snorted. His reasoning didn't make much sense. How could he look the man in the eye when he could barely see out of the eye holes? The whole thing was ridiculous.

They entered the throne room. The flooring changed to smooth stone. The wide room had pillars on each side and what appeared to be a walkway down the center toward a set of stairs covered in a red and gold rug. At the top of the stairs, a man lounged in an oversized chair, leaning heavily on one side. Guards flanked him on each side. Off to the Pharaoh's left, a woman reclined on an oversized pillow in satin turquoise trimmed in gold with gold tassels on each corner. Her gossamer gown was the same color as the pillow. Gold jewels covered her head and dripped down her shiny black hair down her back. This could only be the Great Royal Wife. The sharp-eyed princess stood behind her watching them approach.

Dane was aware there were numerous people along the sides of the throne room, reclining or standing, but he couldn't get a good look at them with the damn mask on his face.

He and Zephrym paused at the foot of the stairs. Zephrym bowed low, dropping to one knee. The Pharaoh's dark eyes flickered over Dane with a curious glint. Then he looked at Zephrym.

"I have heard the Lord of the Underworld returns to walk our lands," the king said. "Rise, my friend."

Zephrym got to his feet. The Pharaoh did the same, unfolding his tall, lanky frame from the oversized chair. His gold robe fluttered around his ankles, showing off his fine leather sandals. He took the steps down from the elevated dais slowly, his keen eyes on Dane the whole time he descended. When the king paused in front of Dane, he could see the king's eyes were lined in heavy kohl, reminding him of Egyptian paintings he'd seen once at a museum. The colorful headdress had the head of a hissing serpent in the center.

"He looks no more god-like than you, Zephrym," the Pharaoh observed with a quirk of a grin. Then his expression turned serious. "My daughter tells me you travel with a sorceress who used her powers to bring the Omoth back to attack us."

The Great Royal Wife suddenly seemed interested in the conversation. She sat up straighter while Amatta moved from behind her mother to join the Pharaoh in front of Dane.

"She has no power. I told the princess that before," Dane said. Even though she couldn't see his expression, he glared at her.

"The Omoth have returned?" the Great Royal Wife was on her feet now. "Were they responsible for the attack on the village?"

Everyone seemed to be waiting for Dane to reply but he remained silent.

Zephrym cleared his throat. "If you will allow me, your majesty?"

Pharaoh Ra-Sha-Tor gave a nod of his head to continue.

"We have had no confirmations they were responsible, but we suspect they were the ones who destroyed the village, killing most of our people and taking out several of the shops and homes."

"Have you come to collect the dead?" Ra-Sha-Tor asked.

Dane stared back at the man, unintimidated by the king. He had no response and wasn't prepared with one. He glanced at Zephrym, but he merely stood there with his hands limp at his side. Dane shook his head, a slow side-to-side movement that pained him.

"We have long been at war with the Omoth. Then you have come to resurrect them to help us fight the Omoth," the king surmised. "Is that it?"

What was he supposed to say to that? He clenched his hands into fists, his palms suddenly sweaty. His mouth had gone dry. Zephrym gave him an encouraging nod, urging him to answer. But Dane remained mute.

The Pharaoh huffed out a breath as he paced the short length of the walkway in front of Dane. "The Omoth have destroyed our villages and temples. Killed our men and women. We have warred with them for ages. Is that why you've come? To take the dead souls with you?"

Amatta folded her arms over her chest. "He claims to be a mortal man. He would have resurrected my husband had it not been for the attack at the tomb."

"I have no interest in the dead," Dane said.

Even though it was the truth, Zephrym shook his head with such a slight movement, it was imperceptible to anyone but Dane. The man with the squint, as Raza called him, pressed his lips together in a thin line so tight, the corners turned white.

Dane guessed it was the wrong thing to say.

"Then why are you here? Why have you decided to walk the land of the living once more?"

If he didn't know any better, Dane would think the Pharaoh sounded rather belligerent about him being there.

How could he answer the question without giving away the time bender safely tucked into the folds of his…whatever the hell it was he wore.

He sensed a sudden presence, as if it were within him.

Tell him you're here to help him with the final battle against the Omoth.

It was Raza's voice in his head. That unmistakable presence made herself known. Her voice was so clear, it was as if she stood right next to him. He wanted to glance around to see if he could find her, but the mask kept him from moving his head. She had said she would be there to help him. Was this her way of doing that?

Yes, she said. *And, yes, I'm in your head. So, pay close attention.*

Then he did the only thing he could. He repeated what she'd said. "I'm here to help you with the final battle against the Omoth."

Amatta huffed a breath. "My father, how can you believe him?"

He held up his hand. "Silence."

The Pharaoh stared at him, hard and long. He took a step toward Dane, leaning close and peering intently at him through the mask. Almost as though he could see the man beneath, even though he couldn't.

"And how will you do that?"

Tell him after the moon passes over the land, there will be an attack. Tell him you will help him defeat the Omoth once and for all. Say it exactly that way or he won't believe you.

Dane wasn't too keen on having the goddess in his head. "After the moon passes over the land, there will be an attack. I will help you defeat the Omoth once and for all."

The room had fallen silent. Zephrym's expression had turned from one of disgust to one of shock as he looked on. Amatta stared, wide-eyed, at him as the Great Royal Wife joined her.

"The prophecy has come true," the queen said. "This is known."

Another prophecy. Dane thought of the one they faced in wintertime with Skye. He wasn't much of a fan of prophecies.

The Pharaoh remained silent. Dane could swear the man's face drained of color. But only for a moment. He regained his composure quickly.

"What must we do?" the king asked, his voice faint.

He must follow your instructions completely, Raza whispered in his ear. *Those instructions will come the morning of the attack.*

Dane cleared his throat. "You will follow my instructions completely. I will have them for you the morning of the attack. In the meantime, ready your men and anyone who can fight."

Fool. I didn't tell you to say that.

He didn't care. All he wanted was to make sure these people had a fighting chance. If Raza was right, if she was telling the truth and the Omoth *did* attack, then these people needed to be ready.

"As you command, your lordship." The Pharaoh bowed his head. "Zephrym, take the Lord of the Underworld to his temple. See to it his needs are met."

"Of course, your majesty."

Zephrym stepped up next to Dane and took him by the elbow. Dane turned away and allowed the man to lead him from the throne room.

"Can I take this thing off yet?" Dane asked as soon as they were out of the throne room.

"No," Zephrym whispered. "There are too many here."

He's right. Don't take if off yet. You don't want to break the illusion you are, in fact, their Lord of the Underworld.

Raza again. He wanted to shove her out of his head but he had no idea how to do that.

You can't, mortal. She put particular emphasis on the word mortal and then snickered.

He growled low in his throat in response.

Her presence, the one he'd felt before she'd spoken in his head, disappeared.

It was then he realized they were leaving the palace.

"Where are we going?" Dane asked.

"To your temple as his majesty commanded."

"Where is that?"

"In the Garden of the Gods." The man pointed to the garden ahead.

Dane could see four temple roof-tops as they wound their way through the plants and flowers. They paused at one of the temples with the word *Qydos* etched into to the top over the entrance. At the doorway, Zephrym halted.

"This is where I leave you."

Dane jerked the mask off his head and sucked in a deep breath of fresh air, filling his lungs and expelling them and cleansing them. Fresh air had never tasted to good.

Zephrym started back up the path, leaving Dane alone in the slash of shadowy sunlight on the temple steps.

"Wait, Zephrym," he called. "You're leaving me here?"

He paused, nodded. "This is where you'll stay now, *Qydos.*"

"Instead of the palace?" Dane asked. "These are better accommodations?"

"It is your temple, your lordship."

The man gave him a wave and then hurried up the path. He disappeared in the foliage. Dane sighed. He'd been kicked out of the palace for being a god. Go figure.

Tucking the mask under his arm, he ascended the steps and entered the temple.

In the center, under a shaft of golden light, was an eight-foot statue of Qydos, Lord of the Underworld. It bore an eerie and remarkable resemblance…to him.

Chapter 9
Punishment in the Quarry

Skye dropped another stone into the basket and watched as one of the children, barefoot, skinny, dirty, tired, hurried away with it. She scanned the area, looking for guards and slave lords. They roamed the quarry, whips in hand looking for workers who weren't working. Or workers who merely displeased them.

She watched the movement of everyone around her, including Hepsheba. The woman was busy chiseling out another brick. With one more quick glance around, Skye pinpointed the location of the guards. They were all interested in others.

That's when she used the corner tip of the chisel to try and pry the manacles off her wrists.

It didn't take Hepsheba long to realize what she was doing. Her eyes went wide and she scooted closer to her, lowing her voice to a roughened whisper.

"Have you gone mad, girl?"

"Maybe," Skye said with a nod. "Maybe I have."

"If you're caught—"

"I'm aware."

She knew all too well what the slave lord would do to her if he saw her trying to break free. In the short time she'd been in the quarry, she'd seen a man beaten to death with the whip lashing. Even when the man fell unconscious, the slave lord hadn't stopped. She knew the same fate would befall her. But it was a chance she was willing to take. She had to get the hell out of there.

And if it worked, and she was able to break through her chains, she'd be taking Hepsheba with her. Maybe even find her daughter and granddaughter and break them free, too. Maybe even start a rebellion in the quarry.

Hepsheba busied her hands with chiseling another brick. "He's looking this way."

She heard the urgency in the old woman's voice. Her heart pounded hard as she stopped trying to break free and went back to carving out another stone.

A gong sounded three times, echoing through the quarry. Hepsheba put down her chisel and got to her feet. She motioned for Skye to do the same. She dropped the tool and stood.

"What is it?" Skye whispered.

"Meal time."

At the thought of food, her stomach rumbled.

All around the quarry, men and women moved into a single-file line and started walking toward the front entrance. Skye and Hepsheba fell in step with them. No one spoke. All the faces Skye scanned were solemn. Fatigue sagged their shoulders. Sweat dampened their tattered and dirty tunics. Their pants were frayed. Most were barefoot. There were a few lucky enough to have sandals, but even those were near worn to nothing.

A pang of sorrow went through her at the sight of it all. Sorrow and fury. She had to find a way to help these people. Dane would help, if she could get to him. If they branded him a god, perhaps there was something he could do.

As they neared the front of the line, she could see the slaves cupping their hands. They were getting nothing but a splash of water in them. That wasn't nearly enough water for these scorching temperatures. The food, if it could be called that, was nothing more than a disgusting gruel ladled into a wooden bowl and passed out after the splash of water.

Hepsheba took the water, giving the guard who dumped it in her hands a grateful nod. When it was Skye's turn, she looked the guard in the eye and shook her head.

"No, thank you."

Everyone stopped, turned, and stared at her.

She ignored them, passing on the water. She knew it was probably a mistake but she wasn't going to slurp water from her dirty hands. She had standards. She moved on to the food. The bowl of gruel was shoved into her hands. She stared down at the disgusting gray matter, trying to decide what it was. The smell was less than appetizing. There were no utensils.

As she looked around, she saw most of them drinking from the bowl. A few used their hands to scoop it out of the bowl and into their mouth.

This was no way to live.

Hepsheba moved to her side. "It's the only meal we get. You best eat."

"The only one?" Skye looked back down at the lumpy gray matter.

The woman nodded. She drank from the bowl, finishing it. She wiped her mouth with the edge of her sleeve. Then handed the empty bowl off to one of the guards.

Skye would rather starve than eat whatever it was. She gave Hepsheba her bowl. "You take it."

The woman's eyes went wide. She shook her head and shoved Skye's hands away. "It is forbidden. This is known."

"But I don't want it. You should have my portion."

"No." She backed away.

"You, there!" one of the guards bellowed.

Hepsheba put her hands up as if in surrender and bowed her head. Skye saw the guard heading right for them. She pulled the bowl back from Hepsheba and suppressed a groan.

But the guard wasn't looking at her. He was looking at Hepsheba.

Oh, shit.

"You accepted an extra offering," he accused.

Anger seared through Skye. "No, she didn't."

His dark gaze turned to her, looked her up and down with disdain.

"I tried to give it to her, but she refused."

Hepsheba sucked air in through her teeth. Her head came up as she looked at Skye. Sudden tears glittered in her eyes and Skye knew she had made a grave error.

But if it meant she took the punishment instead of the old woman, she would accept that. She would take the lashings and then she would find a way to make him pay.

The guard jerked the bowl out of her hands and tossed it to the ground. The gray gruel oozed to the ground like an over-thickened oatmeal. His hand clamped around her upper arm. His fingers dug into her flesh. He dragged her away. Wide eyes in dirty faces followed her and the guard.

But Skye held her head high. She was not going to let them defeat her.

And then she saw where he led her. There were two poles with ropes attached. Fear clawed up her throat. Dark pinpricks flickered through her vision as the blood rushed from her head in a whoosh. She bit back the bark of terror that wanted to erupt.

When they arrived, the manacles were taken off her wrists. The other guards and slave lords joined in as if it was the best thing that had happened all day. Her wrists were tied with the ropes. Her arms were pulled straight out. Skye was dimly aware of the gathering crowd.

She couldn't focus on that. She could only focus on what was about to happen. The slave lord stood behind her, his shadow elongated in front of her from the sun at their backs.

She watched as he uncurled his whip, the tip hitting the ground.

"Let this be a reminder to those of you who think to share your rations. It is forbidden. It has always been forbidden. It will continue to be forbidden."

Skye inhaled a deep breath, closed her eyes and waited.

The first strike hit her across her back where the others had. She clenched her fists so tight, what was left of her nails dug into her palms.

The second one hit her. Refusing the cry out, she bit her lip so hard she tasted blood. Her knees buckled. Her wrists took the brunt of her sagging weight. The rope cut into her skin.

The third one hit her. She squeezed her eyes shut. Hot tears leaked out.

Then they untied her wrists. She collapsed to the ground. Her weak legs were unable to sustain her weight any longer.

It had been more painful than she had ever imagined.

"Throw her in the pit."

It was the last thing she remembered before she passed out from the pain.

Chapter 10
Death Pit

Gooseflesh rose on every inch of exposed skin as Dane stared up at the statue. The carved likeness was much like his own face right down to the square chin. No wonder Princess Amatta thought he was Lord of the Underworld.

"The likeness is uncanny, isn't it? I was surprised, too."

Raza's voice rang out in the hollow space of the temple. She moved from behind the statue to stand next to it, looking up at it with admiration.

"I can't stay here. I have to find someone."

Dane turned toward the opening. He brought out the time bender from the folds of his clothes and glanced down at it. The readout was still very faint. Mud was still embedded in the crevices around the screen. One day had already passed. They had two more left before it would reset itself and then they could, hopefully, time jump again.

"The one they think is a sorceress?" She chuckled, as if the thought of Skye being a sorceress was a source of amusement.

He halted, turned his head slowly to look at the goddess over his shoulder. "What do you know about her? Where is she? Where did they take her?"

"So many questions." She exhibited a bored yawn. "I only saw her when she was with you. I don't know much about her and I don't know where she is."

Hope rose in him. "Can you find her?"

"I could."

He clutched the time bender in his fist and turned fully to face her. "Will you?"

She sighed and closed her eyes. "I see her. She's in the quarry."

"What quarry?"

But the goddess ignored him as she clucked her tongue. "Naughty girl. Now she's using her chisel to try to pry the manacles off her wrists."

He smiled. At least she wasn't going down without a fight.

"Oh. Oh, dear, that's not good."

"What is it?"

"They're taking her to the center of the quarry." She paused, swallowed hard. Her eyes flickered open. Dane could see the worry in them.

"What happened? Where is she?"

"She displeased the slave lord. He whipped her and tossed in the Death Pit."

Whipped? His fist clenched tighter around the time bender until his muscles ached. "What is the Death Pit?"

"It's where they put the slaves who misbehave. They leave them there to die. No food. No water. No nothing."

The blood drained from his head. He swayed on his feet as he thought of Skye in a place as horrid as that. All because of the color of her hair.

"I need to find her. Where is this place? Can you take me there?"

"You cannot leave this place," the goddess said. "You made a promise to the king."

"I made no promise to the king."

"You did. You said you would help him defeat the Omoth. The Omoth plan to attack in the morning."

"That's *his* problem." He started for the opening again and had almost reached it when he felt something grab hold of him and stop him. He couldn't move.

"I cannot allow you to leave this place," Raza said. "I need you. So does the king and his people."

Dane clenched his jaw. He wanted to turn around and glare at her, but he couldn't even move his head. Raza moved to stand in front of him, her eyes glittering with determination.

"I have nothing to do with their fight," he said. "You're the one with the magic. Not me."

"But they think it's you. They won't accept my help."

"Why not?" he demanded.

"Because they don't believe in the Goddess of Balance." She thumbed at her chest. "The Omoth are a warrior people. They are determined to kill every last one of the Hammu here."

"Why?"

"For no other reason than they hate them. Their very existence is an offense to the Omoth."

Dane understood. There were enough people like that back home with a great hatred for each other. So much so, they were willing to commit genocide.

He could not turn his back on these people. He had to help them.

But he also had to find a way to help Skye. His promise was to William Ransom and himself to protect her from harm. So far, in this land, he wasn't doing that great of a job.

"I'll do it on one condition."

She lifted one eyebrow. "And that is?"

"You find Skye and get her out of the Death Pit."

She pressed her lips together but at last nodded. "Very well."

The goddess disappeared leaving him alone in the temple with the statue.

~ ⧗ ~

The pain was almost too much. Skye came to sometime later, curled in a heap with the sun beating down on her. She repositioned but it did nothing to alleviate the heat pounding through her. She lifted her head and saw she was not alone.

There were several others with her in this place. Their tired, sunburned faces peered at her with a mix of horror and sorrow. She knew her back must be a shredded mess. She could feel the tightness of the skin where she'd been whipped and the trickle of blood. The back of her tunic—what was left of it—was tattered and damp. No doubt with sweat and blood.

Overhead, a large gaping hole. The noonday sun shone straight down. There was no shade. She used her hand to shield her eyes from the sun as she peered up into the bright light. She saw nothing but the brilliant orb and the edge of the hole.

Take her to the pit.

It was the last thing she remembered before she passed out. She imagined they hauled her up as if she were nothing but a rag doll and dropped her down in this hell hole of a place. As she imagined it, every bone in her body began to ache. She should check for other injuries, but what was the point? She was likely going to die in this place. Dane had no idea where she was or how to find her. They had been separated for nearly a day.

And they were inching closer to the time bender resetting itself and allowing them to jump again.

She hoped he found his way to her by then. She knew he wouldn't leave without her.

But he if he couldn't find her, and if he left without her, she couldn't blame him. He would have to make that difficult decision. She idly wondered what she would do if she were in that situation. It wasn't something they had talked about. They both had assumed, unwisely, they would stick together.

Things looked bleak for her, though.

She managed to get to a sitting position and scoot back from the center of the pit. All eyes kept trained on her as she moved. Unfortunately, no one got out of the unrelenting sun. Dizzying fatigue pushed through her. She couldn't sit upright so she fell to her side, her head pillowed on her arm. The last thing she wanted to do was lay on her destroyed back. Wasn't it enough she had sweat trickling into the open wound?

Tears threatened. The hot pinpricks of them beat against her eyes. She refused to let them fall. She would not allow her emotions to overcome her. Not here. She had to have hope Dane would somehow find her and get her out of here.

A shadow appeared at the edge of the pit. It was enough to garner everyone's attention. Even hers. She glanced upward, saw the outline of a head and shoulders. The sun blotted out the face, leaving nothing but the outline.

Then the person swung legs into the pit and jumped down, landing on her feet in the center. She rose to her full height, her keen eyes scanning the small crowd until she came to Skye. Recognition flickered through her gaze.

"The one with the flaming red hair. The one who was branded a sorceress." She gave Skye a little smile.

Skye didn't know this woman. "Who are you?"

"I've been sent to retrieve you." She held her hand out to her. "Come. We must go at once."

"Who sent you?" Suspicion laced Skye's words.

The woman rolled her eyes. "Your traveling companion. Now come."

Hope flared bright and hot as the sun inside Skye. She took the woman's hand and let her help her to her feet.

"Wait. What about them?" She nodded to the others in the pit.

She gave them a cursory glance. "They're here for a reason," the woman said.

"We can't leave them," Skye said.

"We can't save them, either." The woman took her hand again. "You're as difficult as he is."

Before Skye could reply, they moved from the depths of the pit to outside the quarry in a flash of light. It was enough to make Skye queasy. She doubled-over, clutching her stomach and groaning.

"What did you do to me?"

"Oh, I forget you little mortals can't sift like I can."

"Sift?" She groaned again and collapsed to her knees.

"You need medical attention." The woman said it more as an observation.

Skye dry heaved in answer.

"If you'll allow me to help?" the woman asked.

Skye could only nod agreement. The woman placed a hand on her shoulder.

And then she, mercifully, passed out.

Chapter 11
To Tell the Truth

When Skye came to, she peeled her eyes open and stared at an unfamiliar ceiling. She did a quick inspection of her body and found she was no longer in pain. In fact, it seemed as though her injuries had fully healed.

The last thing she remembered was the strange woman rescuing her from the pit and leaving behind the others. She had moved from there to outside the quarry in what seemed like a flash of light that left her ill.

"There now. All better, eh?"

It was the woman who had saved her. Skye sat up to get a good look at her surroundings. This was not the pit or the quarry or even the little room she'd been tossed into with Malika. This was a different place altogether. The room was plain with no decoration whatsoever. She was on a narrow bed with nothing more than a scratching blanket. A light flickered from a lamp on the bedside table.

"Where am I?"

"Relax. I brought you to a place that could help you." The woman moved to stand in front her. She gave her a once-over and then nodded. "And you look much better than when I found you. You'll want this." She handed her a clean tunic.

Skye took it from her, still wary of the woman. "Thanks. Where is Dane?"

"Ah, yes. You'll be wanting to get back to him soon, I'm sure. He's fine for now. Ra-Sha-Tor and his Great Royal Wife—" she rolled her eyes as she said it "—thinks he's their savior."

"Because they think he's the Lord of the Underworld," Skye said. She assumed Ra-Sha-Tor was the Pharaoh.

"And we both know he's not. Just as we know you're not a sorceress." Her gaze flickered over her, pausing on her hair. A smile creased her mouth. "Maybe you tell me who you two are and what you're doing in my realm."

"We're passing through. That's all." She clutched the clean tunic between her hands, unsure how much to tell her. "Maybe you tell me who *you* are."

"Oh, is this let's make a deal again?" She expelled an annoyed sigh. "Fine, then. I am Raza, Goddess of Balance. I'm here to restore order to this little corner of the universe."

"I've never heard of you." Skye wasn't sure why she wanted to needle the woman. She'd saved her life and healed her wounds, after all.

Raza gave her a thin-lipped smile that didn't reach her eyes. "It doesn't matter if you've heard of me or not. What matters is that you and your companion have upset the order of things here. I can't have that. But since the damage is already done, and since the Hammu think he's been brought here to resurrect the dead and save them from the Omoth..." She paused, looking pleased. "Well, that's something I can work with."

"Who are the Hammu?"

"The indigenous people of this land."

"And the Omoth?"

"The ones who want to wipe them out. Oh, not all of them. Some just want to relocate them," Raza said.

Skye understood what she meant but she was still unclear on something else. "How does being here with Dane mess things up?"

"Because you're not supposed to be here, are you, now? Neither of you belong here."

The goddess was right. As Skye sat clutching the tunic, an idea formed. "You're right. Neither of us belong here. So maybe you can help us get back to where we *do* belong."

A dark thin brow lifted. "And why would I do that?"

"Because you want to restore order and balance," Skye suggested.

She laughed. "I like you, Skye. You're smart. And you're right. I do want to restore order and balance. Why don't you tell me where you two belong and I'll see if I can help?"

That was a difficult question, wasn't it? Even Skye wasn't sure how to explain it to her. Not only was it the time traveling she would have to explain, but also the *how* of the time traveling. And she wasn't even sure they were in the same linear timeline as when they left. How could she describe that?

She and Dane had been through so much together since her parents were murdered, she didn't even know where to begin. She chewed the inside of her lip as she decided what to say and how to say it.

"Well?" Raza asked.

She decided to blurt it out. "We're time travelers."

A sense of relief expelled from her as she said the words. She had no idea how good it would feel to tell *someone* about their exploits. Raza stared at her as though she'd grown a second head, though. Not a good sign.

"Time travelers? Not possible." She shook her head, dismissing the thought.

"It *is* possible. I swear to you. My father built a device that allows us to move through time." And space, but she wasn't one-hundred-percent sure that was accurate. She and Dane had discussed it briefly but they had no concrete evidence that was, in fact, happening.

"I don't believe you."

"You said yourself we don't belong here."

"If you had a device to time travel, then why do you need my help?" She propped her hands on her slender hips.

"It's faulty. It won't send us back home, so we're stuck traveling in time in the hopes we can get back."

"But you never do."

"No and this is the…" She paused. Scotland, wintertime, the Citadel, now here. "This is the fourth place we've landed."

"Hm." She still sounded unconvinced.

"I can prove it to you," Skye said.

"Then do it."

"Dane has the device. Take me to him and I'll ask him to show it to you."

Again, that thin brow lifted in question and disbelief. "He has the device."

"Yes." Skye gave an emphatic nod.

All she needed was Raza to take her to Dane. Once they were back together everything would be fine.

"Kronos is the only one I know who can control time," Raza said. "And he is a god."

"Are you saying you don't believe me?" Skye said.

"I'm saying I don't believe there is a device that can alter time."

She sighed, frustration edging through her. "If you would just take me to him, I can have him show you."

"Fine."

With a huff, she waved her arms and they flashed away. Skye didn't have a chance to prepare herself before it happened. Skye crashed against a hard surface with a grunt, bashing her elbow on the floor. Her stomach clenched with that queasy feeling she got earlier. Before she could process any of that, though, two firm hands gripped her by the upper arms and hoisted her to her feet. Before she could react,

Dane pulled her into a fierce hug. It was so out of character for him, it startled her and took her several seconds to hug him back.

Her queasy stomach was suddenly forgotten when she was wrapped in his arms. His warmth enveloped her, giving her the comfort she needed. When they broke apart, she realized they were in some type of temple. The eight-foot-statute of the Lord of the Underworld behind him did not escape her notice. The statue looked a lot like Dane.

"Thank god you're all right." He gave her a good once over. "Raza said they whipped you."

"I'm all healed." She twisted to show him her back and the shredded tunic. "And it's nice to see you, too." She took a step back and looked at his attire, or lack thereof. "What the hell is this?" She wagged a finger at him.

"Zephrym made me."

"It's even better with the mask," Raza said, sounding well pleased.

"What mask?" Skye asked.

"It doesn't matter. Raza, thanks for your help."

"Oh, sure. Now show me the device."

Dane's gaze flickered back to Skye. "You told her?"

"I think she can help us get home," she said. "But she doesn't believe we have a time traveling device."

He took her by the arm and pulled her aside, away from the goddess. He lowered his voice. "I don't think you should have told her."

"Why not? She made it clear we don't belong here. We've upset the order of things in this world," Skye whispered back.

"Realm," she corrected. "And I can still hear you both." She stomped over to them and held out her hand. She wiggled her fingers in a *gimme* gesture. "Show me."

Skye gave him an encouraging nod. He pulled the time bender from the folds whatever it was he wore. He held it in his palm so she could see. When she reached for it, he closed his fingers and snatched his hand away.

"Sorry, goddess. It stays with me."

"You don't trust me?"

"I don't trust anyone."

She gave him a look of disgust. "Fine, then. At least hold it closer so I can get a better look."

He did as she asked. Raza bent to peer down at the device. "It's a strange little thing. What, exactly, does it do?"

"It bends time around us," Dane said.

"How does it work?" she wanted to know.

"You press the button." He pointed to the black button still caked with dried mud.

"And this?" She pointed to the screen.

"It's supposed to show the date of the time you're going to," Skye replied.

She stared at it a long quiet moment, then stood straight. "I will consult Kronos." Before either of them could reply, she disappeared.

"Who's Kronos?" Dane asked, his voice echoing in the temple.

"The God of Time."

Chapter 12
The Consequences of Time Travel

"Why would she consult the God of Time?" Dane asked.

"Because she hates us?" Skye said flippantly.

He gave her a sour look.

"I hope she can convince him to send us home," Skye added.

When she landed in the temple, she'd dropped the tunic on the floor. Now she snatched it up and walked around behind the statue where he couldn't see her. She whipped off the tattered one and pulled on the new. As she came around the front of the statue, she noticed the Anubis mask. She let the tattered cloth flutter to the ground and picked up the mask.

"Is this the mask Raza referred to?"

"It is." Dane paced the length of the small temple, the time bender clutched in his hand.

She stuck the mask on her face and immediately regretted it. The stench was unbearable. She yanked it off, gagging.

"God, that's awful. You wore that?"

"I was forced to when I met the Pharaoh." He halted his pacing then and met her gaze. "What happened to you? Where did they take you?"

"Thanks to Princess Amatta," Skye paused and scowled at the mention of her name, "I was thrown into the slave barracks. At least, that's what I think they were. This morning, they took me to the quarry. They're using slaves to chisel bricks from the limestone to build their pyramid."

"That's what they're building?"

"It has to be. The walls slant upward like a pyramid. I met a woman there in the quarry. Her name is Hepsheba. This Pharaoh is stealing people from mountain villages and turning them into slaves."

A look of horror and disgust flickered over his face.

"We have to do something," Skye added.

"What can we do?"

"I don't know. You're the Lord of the Underworld. Or maybe get Raza to do something about it."

"I think Raza does what she wants. She made me promise to help the Hammu defeat the Omoth. Tell me why they whipped you."

"Oh. That." She frowned at the memory. "I tried to give Hepsheba my daily rations. Apparently, that's forbidden. So, they whipped me in the center of the quarry and tossed me in the pit."

"They call it the Death Pit," Dane said.

She thought of the people left behind and knew they were going to die. It pained her to think about it. Pained her to know they had been left behind when she had been rescued.

"I know that look, Skye. You want to save them, too."

"I want to save them all," she corrected. "We can't just leave them here."

"We have to," he said. "Raza said it herself. Our arrival has upset the balance of this place."

Skye chewed on her thumbnail. "Do you think that's the case for the other places we've been?"

He shrugged. "Hard to say." He moved closer to her, took her hand. "Skye, I'm sorry. I should have been there for you. I promised I would and I failed you."

"No, you didn't. We can't control what the inhabitants of whatever land we end up in do. All we can do is control our own actions," she said. She glanced down at his still-clenched fist. "What about the time bender? Has it reset?"

"Not yet. And the readout is still faint."

His tone suggested he wasn't certain it would ever reset. She didn't like this tone. But she had to accept it. She had to know there was a possibility that they would be stuck there— or somewhere—forever.

Unless Kronos decided to take pity on them and send them home. "What do we do now?" she asked. "Hang around here indefinitely?"

"This is where I was brought after the meeting with the Pharaoh. We're still within the palace grounds. This temple is in the gardens. I suppose it's my new home until the big battle."

"What big battle?"

"When the moon passes over the land, there will be an attack. That's what Raza said."

"And she knows this for sure?"

"She's a goddess, isn't she? She has to know everything that goes on."

"She called this her realm," Skye said, remembering their earlier conversation. "Like there is more than one realm."

Dane thought a moment, his thumb brushing her palm. It sent a tingling sensation up her arm and prickled the back of her neck. She liked it. A lot.

"Remember what Thomas said?"

He'd told them both that the way the time bender bent time it could open parallel universes. *Really, there's no telling where and when the person using the time bender will end up.*

"Yes, and I've been thinking about that, too. Do you think it's true?"

"I think it must be. Everything we've experienced has been…different. Not of our world."

"Everything except Scotland," she said. "When we were in that time, it seemed as though we were still…" She paused, trying to find the words.

"In our own time and realm?"

She nodded. "Something like that."

"Maybe this time bender is faultier than we think." He opened his hand and looked down at the offending device. "Maybe it's bending space and time both. Maybe it really is opening those parallel universes. And it's getting worse with every jump."

"And we're sort of stuck in limbo?"

He nodded.

She considered this, chewing on her lower lip. "Then there is a possibility we may never get home." Saying the words aloud made her stomach clench with fear.

"We don't know that."

"We don't know anything," she said. "Thomas was the only one who knew and we can't exactly call him up right now."

He squeezed her hand in reassurance. "We'll think of something."

Raza returned and along with her was a man. He was tall, with salt and pepper wavy hair that brushed his shoulders. His face was covered in a similar salt and pepper beard, neatly trimmed. He glared at them both with bright blue eyes. This had to be the God of Time.

"These are the ones you mentioned?" he asked Raza.

"Yes."

"The ones with the device."

"Yes," Raza said.

Skye didn't like where this was going. She edged closer to Dane.

Kronos closed the gap between them, his eyes narrowed at them both in suspicion. "Let me see it."

"See what?" Dane asked, clearly playing dumb.

"The device Raza told me about."

Skye wanted to tell him not to show it to him. But she didn't know how to communicate that without verbalizing it. The two of them hadn't exactly figured out mind-speak. Dane gave him a toothy grin.

"I'm afraid I don't know what you're talking about."

Kronos backhanded him. It was so unexpected, Skye gasped as soon as it happened. Dane stumbled backward a step or two before he regained his footing and his composure. His expression went from surprise to anger in two-point-three-seconds. He drew back his arm, his hand in a fist, ready to strike. Skye reached for him, wrapped her hands around his upper arm to stop him.

"No, Dane," she whispered. Because hitting a god in the face would be the worst thing he could do.

He glanced at her, met her gaze, and realized he'd balled his hand in a fist. He relaxed his hand, flexing his fingers.

"Just show him," she said, her voice still low.

He still had the device in his other hand. He held it out, showing Kronos the small device. When he tried to take it, Dane closed his hand and snatched it away. Kronos gave him a look that could melt rubber.

"Raza speaks true then. You have been tinkering with time travel."

"It was an accident," Skye said. "We didn't intend to do it. It just happened."

He gave her a sour look. "Nothing *just happens*, young lady."

She pressed her lips together, unsure how to respond to that. The heated look he gave her made her shrink back, as though she were a child chastised by a grown-up.

"It is forbidden to bend time, as you call it," Kronos said. "And, so, a price must be paid."

Next to her, Dane tensed. "What sort of price?"

Kronos' answer was to snap his fingers. Before Skye knew what was happening, she was hurtled through time and space. She landed on the hard earth and skidded several feet in a shower of dirt. She had dirt in her hair, her face, her mouth, her eyes. When she finally came to a halt, she looked up into the shocked face of Hepsheba.

She'd been returned to the slave quarry.

~ ⧖ ~

"What did you do with her? Bring her back," Dane demanded.

"It is her punishment. The Hammu put her in the slave quarry for a reason. I merely returned her there."

Anger seared through him. He clenched his fist tighter around the device and turned his fury on Raza.

"This is your doing," he said.

"No," she replied. "It's *your* doing."

"And you will be punished, too." He lifted his arms in a flourish.

Raza stopped him. "What are you going to do?"

Kronos turned his laser-eyed gaze on her. "You brought me here to show me and now I've seen. I cannot let him go unpunished."

"I brought you here because you didn't believe he had a device." She looked a Dane. Regret lined her features. "I need him still. I can't balance order and chaos without him."

"He is a *mortal*," Kronos said. "You said it yourself."

"Yes, I know, but…" She paused, still looking apologetic. "Pharaoh expects him to help defeat the Omoth."

Kronos sighed. "You and your little projects, Raza. Need I remind you that none of this would be happening if you hadn't interfered in the first place?"

She pressed her lips together in a thin line. "No, you needn't remind me, Kronos. I need Dane to finish what was started with the Hammu. Once we do that, then you can do whatever you need to do with him."

He stared at her a long, silent moment. "Very well, then. But once the Omoth are handled and the Hammu are back in their rightful place, I *will* return." He gave Dane a searing glance before disappearing.

As soon as he was gone, Raza blew out a relieved breath. Dane was having none of it. He charged her, shoved her against the wall with his arm on her throat. Her eyes flew wide as she clawed at him to release her.

"This is all your doing?"

She gasped for breath. "It was…a mistake."

"What was?" he demanded.

"War…with the Omoth. An accident."

He released her and stepped back with his hands clenched into fists. The last thing he needed was the goddess's death on his hands. "You lied to me. To us."

"I'm sorry but when I saw the way the Hammu reacted to you, I knew it was my chance to fix what had been wronged." She spread her hands in forgiveness. "It's my only chance to bring balance and order back to these two peoples. If I don't…" She paused, shuddered.

"Then what?"

"Then I'll be executed." As she said the last word, she swallowed hard. "Will you help still?"

"I don't exactly have a choice, do I?" And he hated that. "Skye was sent back to the quarry. I need to go after her."

He headed for the exit of the temple, but Raza grabbed him by the arm and stopped him. "Skye is stronger than you give her credit. She'll be fine."

"She needs me."

"*I* need you. If you leave and Kronos comes back, or—worse—if Zephrym comes looking for you, there will be hell to pay. The sun is about to set."

"You're telling me I have to stay here until morning."

"Yes," she said with a nod.

Dane didn't like that answer but he would accept it for now. While he could agree Skye could likely take care of herself, he didn't like leaving her in that awful place alone. He would find a way to get back to her before this was all over.

"What are we supposed to do before this attack?"

Raza gave him a half smile. "We wait."

Chapter 13
Insurrection

Hepsheba hauled Skye to her feet, brushing away most of the dirt from her hair, face, and clothes. Questions lined her sun-warmed face. Questions Skye knew she wanted to ask. Questions Skye had no idea how to answer.

"The slave lord threw you in the pit." The old woman pressed her aged fingers to her lips, as though speaking it aloud would conjure the slave lord.

"He did," she agreed. "I got out."

That was all the woman needed to know. There was no need to tell her about Raza or Kronos.

"And your back… I saw them whip you several times. The skin on your back was flayed and bleeding."

Nodding, Skye took her by the arm and led her toward the rock face where they'd spent so much time chiseling bricks. "You're right."

"I don't understand."

"You don't need to," Skye said.

"Why did you come back?"

Skye plopped down on the ground and took up her chisel. "I came back to help you."

It wasn't far from the truth. Skye didn't like knowing the woman was chiseling bricks from the rock, destroying her hands and fingers, not to mention her back. After sitting in the hunched position for several hours, it was painful.

Skye noticed the manacles on the woman's wrists had left them raw and bleeding. It pained her to see that knowing there wasn't much she could do for her. She had hoped Raza would help her and Dane get out of this time, but instead the goddess tattled on them to Kronos. How could she do that?

"You there."

It was one of the slave lords. Hepsheba watched him head towards them and nudged Skye. Skye kept on chiseling away at the rock.

"I said, you there. Girl."

"He's talking to you," Hepsheba whispered.

Skye dropped her chisel and turned to face the man. He was tall, broad-shouldered, ugly. His skin was weather from years of being in the sun. His face a roadmap of wrinkles and his mouth drawn down in a permanent grimace. Slowly, she unfolded her body and got to her feet to face him.

At some point, Skye decided she wasn't afraid of him. She wasn't afraid of any of them because she knew she didn't belong here. No matter what happened to her, she would leave this place soon with Dane because she had faith the faulty time bender would, indeed, still work.

"Yeah?" Skye asked, meeting the man's gaze.

She heard the rustle of material and the clink of metal behind her and knew Hepsheba got to her feet, too. She could see movement in her peripheral vision and knew the others in the area had stopped working to openly gape at Skye facing off with the slave lord.

"You were thrown in the pit, were you not?" His booming voice echoed through the quarry, garnering more attention.

"I was." Skye nodded affirmative, her voice even and calm. "What about it?"

His hand whipped out and gripped her upper arm, his fingers digging into her flesh. "No one escapes the Death Pit. So, how did *you*?"

She steeled herself for what was to come, took a deep breath, exhaled it. "With a little help from my friend."

She heard Hepsheba's sharp intake of breath. Probably because Skye had dared to talk back to the slave lord.

The man's eyes narrowed. "Who is this friend?"

Skye decided it was time to name drop. "The Lord of the Underworld. Perhaps you've heard of him?"

He growled his response. "You lie."

"Do I?" she challenged.

Frustrated, he shoved her aside and turned his ire on Hepsheba. "Did you help her?"

The woman shook her head and backed away. Her eyes were wide with fear. But the slave lord didn't accept her answer. He uncoiled his whip.

"You lie. I think you helped her."

Something inside Skye snapped. She'd had it with this guy and all the rest of them.

He raised his hand, ready to strike. Skye jumped between the two of them and raised her arm just as he lashed out the whip. The end coiled around her wrist, leaving stinging pain behind. Skye took his momentary surprise and wrapped her hand around the whip. She gave it a mighty jerk and yanked it from his hand.

When she did, she heard a collective gasp behind her. She wanted them to see. She wanted them to know they could fight back. There were more of them than the slave lords and guards. With the right motivation, they could overtake them and get out of the quarry.

With a calm she didn't know she possessed she slowly coiled the rest of the whip around her hand. She tried not to see the bits of skin and blood stained on the leather.

"She didn't help me. None of these people did. I'll thank you to leave them alone…" She leaned closer. "And I'll let the Lord of the Underworld know you threatened an innocent woman."

He wasn't the least bit intimidated, not even with threatening him by dropping Dane's newly acquired title. He glared right back at her.

"You'll give me that whip now, girl."

"No, I won't. You've beat enough people with it."

He snarled. "That will be your last mistake. The Grand Master will hear of this and you will be punished."

He stalked away, leaving Skye holding the whip still wrapped around her hand. Blood oozed from her wrist as she slowly uncoiled the thing.

"The Grand Master will kill you," Hepsheba said, her voice a shaky whisper. Worry lines creased her forehead.

"He won't have a chance to," she replied coolly.

"Why not?"

"Because we're getting out of here." She spun to face Hepsheba. "All of us."

The woman's face paled as she shook her head. "You are mad, girl."

"You're right. I *am* mad and getting madder." She noticed all the wide-eyed faces gaping at her as though she'd lost her mind. "We can defeat them and get out of here."

"How?" Hepsheba asked.

"You'll have to trust me. Do you?"

The woman glanced at the others. They exchanged a silent communication and then finally Hepsheba nodded. "Yes."

Skye smiled, excited to be leading them into a rebellion. Though how she was going to do that, she hadn't decided yet. "Good. Now, let's get started."

Her mind worked fast as she glanced around at the small group. Two men and Hepsheba. They all had chisels in their hands. Chisels that could be used as weapons.

"First, we're going to find your daughter and granddaughter," Skye said to Hepsheba.

"And then my daughter?" one of the men said, hopeful.

"And my son?" the other added.

"Yes," Skye nodded. "We're going to find them all."

"No," Hepsheba whispered.

"No? Why not?" Skye asked.

The woman pointed at something behind her. Skye turned and there was the ugly slave lord and another man who was clearly dressed better and hadn't been sweating in the sun all day. His long pants were dirty, though, as though he'd been kneeling in the mud, and his black boots had a coating of dust. His tunic was covered in dirt. He wore a red cape that billowed out behind him as he walked. This had to be the Grand Master. She sighed. At least she still had the whip.

But the Grand Master had a sword and a dagger at his belt.

This was likely not going to end well. She may have dug herself into a hole she couldn't get out.

"Great," she muttered. Now what?

"Do you really know the Lord of the Underworld?" one of the men whispered.

"Yes," Skye said.

"Then you better pray and pray hard, girl, he comes to your rescue," Hepsheba said.

Skye took a deep breath and faced her newest enemy.

Chapter 14
Quarry Raiders

She should really be afraid of these men. Skye wasn't exactly sure what had come over her, but she had decided she wasn't going to take it and she wasn't going to watch these innocent people suffer anymore. Hepsheba and the others moved behind her, as if she were the shield that guarded them from evil. She stood her ground when they stopped in front of her.

The Grand Master looked her up and down with disdain. "This is the one? This little girl?"

"She took my whip," the slave lord complained.

"You whine like a mule," the Grand Master replied. "And how did this little girl take your whip from you?"

Skye lifted an eyebrow as she glanced between the two of them. She wanted to laugh at the way the Grand Master talked down to the man.

He did what any man would do to save face. He lied. "She overpowered me."

Skye snorted.

The Grand Master's gaze snapped to her. "She did, did she?"

She almost laughed. Instead, she kept it bottled inside and the whip firmly in her hand. She wasn't about to give it up. His gaze flickered from her face to her hand where she held the thing, then back to her face.

"Go to your post, Augustus," he said. "I will deal with her."

"But my whip—"

"Do as I order."

She lifted her brows to her hairline as she watched the slave lord stomp away. The Grand Master waited until the man was out of earshot before he took a step closer to her, lowering his voice to sound more menacing and terrifying.

"Here's what is going to happen, little girl. You'll hand me that whip. Then I'll punish you with it and throw you back into the Death Pit where you will stay while you slowly starve to death," he said.

She smirked. "I don't think so."

"No?"

"That's what I said. No."

He smirked back. "And why is that, little girl?"

"First of all, stop calling me little girl." She let the whip unwind. The tip plopped into the dirt by her feet. "Second of all, the only one using this weapon is me."

She had no clue how to use a whip. Either she was going to hit her mark or she was going to flay herself alive. She did what instinct told her to do. She stepped back—she felt Hepsheba and the others behind her scatter—and raised the whip in a wide arc over her head, letting it lash out at the Grand Master.

He ducked and drew his sword.

At least she missed smacking herself with the strap of leather.

And suddenly she felt like Indiana Jones standing there holding her whip while the man showed off his fancy sword-twirling.

A shout rose up from somewhere in the quarry garnering the Grand Master's attention. They all looked toward the west, where the sun had dipped toward the horizon. Coming over the ridge into the quarry, shrouded in darkness, were invaders.

Skye's heart leapt into her throat. This had to be the invasion Dane mentioned to her. With the Grand Master distracted, she knew this was their chance. She spun toward Hepsheba and the others.

"Now's our chance. Come on!"

She took off at a dead run. They followed, their manacles clinking as they ran with her.

Pandemonium broke out in the quarry. Screams could be heard. Screams of fear and terror and death.

"My daughter…" Hepsheba choked.

Skye didn't pause to answer. When she saw a slave lord and one of the guards heading for her, she slowed to a stop. She fumbled with the whip, trying to use it. It was mostly a useless weapon for her because she hadn't a clue how to wield it.

The two men who had been running with her passed her. They tackled the guard and the slave lord. She could see the flash of some type of weapon one of the men had as he shoved it into the guard's side. The second man took out the slave lord with his fists. With the men down, they stole their weapons and the keys to the manacles off the slave lord. He quickly put the keys to use and released them all.

Skye smiled. "Nice work. Now, let's see who else we can help."

~ ⧗ ~

"The slaves are in open rebellion."

Raza had reappeared as suddenly as she disappeared. Her abrupt arrival startled Dane. He recovered quickly, though.

"Also, there's an uprising in the quarry," she added.

"What does all that mean?" he asked.

"It means your girlfriend may have had something to do with the open rebellion. It means the Omoth have arrived earlier than expected and attacked those in the quarry. It means it's show time." She flashed a bright smile as if this was the best thing ever.

"How do you know all this?" Dane demanded.

She rolled her eyes and thumbed at her chest. "Goddess."

He started for the exit of the temple. "I have to get to Skye."

"Hey, Lord of the Underworld, aren't you forgetting something?"

When he turned to face her, he saw she held the Anubis mask. He shook his head. "No." There was no way he was putting that back on. He needed full movement of his upper body and he needed to be able to see where he was going and what he was doing.

"You said you'd help as the Lord of the Underworld. That was the deal." She held the Anubis mask out to him.

He swore under his breath and snatched the mask. "Fine."

Just as he did, Zephrym arrived. He panted hard, sweat lining his face as though he'd run all the way here. He bent, his hands on his knees as he tried to catch his breath. Raza had melted into the shadows.

"The Omoth are here," Dane said.

The man gave an emphatic nod.

"Then let's go."

"The Pharaoh…has taken his war chariot out himself."

Behind him, he could hear Raza expel an annoyed breath.

"Then we better hurry," Dane said. He motioned to the exit of the temple.

As he stepped out, full on night had descended, cloaking the world in darkness. They were headed to war.

Chapter 15
Balance Comes with a Price

It was a blood bath. Everywhere Skye turned, there were dead slaves, dead slave lords, dead guards. The Omoth cut a path through the middle of the quarry. They knew exactly where they were going and how to get there.

She and her little entourage had engaged in their own battles in an effort to stay alive. It was definitely a fight for survival. They had yet to find the missing children of the two men and Hepsheba. And now that darkness had descended in the quarry, it was difficult to see.

The Omoth had come prepared with torches and swords drawn. They cut down anyone that got in their way. It didn't matter if they were women or children. As several charged toward Skye and her new friends, she knew they couldn't fight them. She motioned for them to halt and duck behind an oversized boulder. They passed by and when they did, she got a good look at one of them.

Yellow-orange torchlight flickered across his features. She covered her mouth to keep from gasping aloud. His face was smashed in, his nose upturned. Two tusks protruded from either side of his mouth. Hair covered his hands and fingers, the nails ending in claws.

This creature was the infamous Omoth? The men who attacked them at the tomb looked nothing like them. Perhaps they were merely the Omoth's army, then?

A flash of light nearly blinded Skye. She shielded her eyes and when the light faded and she could see again, Dane stood before her in that ridiculous Anubis mask.

Relief sputtered through her, though, at the sight of him. Raza was behind him saying something Skye couldn't hear.

Dane lifted his hands in a sweeping motion and the army of creatures blew apart in a shower of blood and guts.

"Your prayers have been answered, girl," Hepsheba said. She nodded toward Dane.

He hadn't seen them yet. She wasn't sure she wanted him to. She, Hepsheba and the two men hunched toward the ground watching as Dane, or Raza rather, took out the invaders. They advanced into the crowd, leaving them behind.

"What should we do?" Hepsheba asked.

"We wait," Skye said. Because she had no doubt Dane would find her. She wanted to stay in one place until all of this was over.

As the words left her lips, the Pharaoh charged onto the battlefield on his chariot led by two black horses. He had his hand raised, a short sword clutched in his fist as he emitted a war cry. He was followed by his own army, the horses trampling what was left of the Omoth army.

A strange silence descended on the quarry. Something about it didn't feel right. Skye got to her feet and peered around the rock to see the Pharaoh, Dane, and Raza facing off with several other men.

"Your army has been destroyed, Caius," the Pharaoh shouted. "The Hammu people are yours no more to torture and maim."

The man in the center, Caius, laughed. "You left your palace unguarded. Your daughter and your Great Royal Wife will be mine before dawn."

This infuriated the Pharaoh. He jumped down from his chariot, shouting another war cry, and charging toward Caius. Swords clashed, the steel glinting in the moonlight and the light of the torches. Dane and Raza stepped back away from the two men fighting, giving them a wide berth.

Behind Caius, his men charged. Pharaoh's army engaged them turning the quarry into a battlefield.

A flash of light like the previous one and then Dane was standing before Skye. He ripped off the Anubis mask and tossed it to the ground.

"We are done here," he said to Raza.

"The battle is not over," she said.

"It is for me and Skye." He reached for her, taking her by the hand and pulling her closer. "We're leaving this place."

"What about our children? You promised to help find them?" Hepsheba demanded.

The two men nodded agreement.

Dane cut Skye a glance. "Please tell me you didn't?"

"I'm sorry, but I did. I want to help them. All of them." She swept her hand to encompass the quarry.

"Not possible." Raza stepped up beside Dane.

"Why not?" Skye demanded.

"Because there is balance and order that must be maintained. It's not their time to be free." She glanced back at the Pharaoh still locked into a battle with the Omoth leader. "I must go to make sure the outcome of this battle is the right one."

She didn't say what that was before she disappeared.

Dane gripped her hand tighter. "Come on. Let's go."

Skye hated knowing she hadn't been able to keep her promise. She had so much wanted to make sure Hepsheba found her daughter and granddaughter. She mouthed the words *I'm sorry* as Dane led her away to the edge of the quarry.

"Where are we going to go? The time bender still has one day to reset, doesn't it?" she asked.

"I don't care where we go as long as it's not here."

They left the battle and the quarry behind but before they put a lot of distance between them, Kronos made another appearance. Dane came to a jarring halt, still holding her hand.

"You two are nothing but trouble," he said. His gaze flickered to Skye and he addressed her. "Do you realize what you've done?"

"I've done nothing."

"You have done more damage today than anything Raza did," he said, his voice dripping disdain.

"And what exactly is that?" Dane wanted to know.

"She gave the slaves hope." Kronos glared at Skye. "One—her—manage to escape." He jabbed his forefinger at her. "Now they will all want to escape."

"They are *slaves*. Stolen from their homes. They deserve to be free." She practically spat the words.

"You do not get to make that decision," Kronos said. "It's not the time for their freedom. Not here. Not yet. Raza has done what she could to restore balance. You, however…" He paused, shook his head. "You destroyed the order of things." Then he turned his glittering, angry gaze on Dane. "And you impersonated a god. Both of you will be punished accordingly."

Dane pulled her closer and started to say something but Skye interrupted.

"We want to go home," she said. "If you send us home, there will be no more time traveling."

He seemed to consider this for a moment, but then shook his head. "I'm afraid that's not possible. The laws of time are clear. You both violated them. As God of Time, I cannot let that go unpunished. Any last words?"

"What sort of punishment?" Dane asked.

He grinned. "A test of survival."

Dane turned to Skye, gripping both her hands in his. "If we're separated, I'll find you."

She memorized his face, met his depthless green eyes and nodded as fear gripped. Her stomach clenched into a tight knot.

"Oh, isn't that sweet?" Kronos rolled his eyes. "If you must stay together, so be it."

Kronos, the God of Time, snapped his fingers.

The world beneath their feet fell out from under them. The last thing Skye remembered seeing was Dane's face and then darkness.

Epilogue
Secret Mission

Present Day, Arlington, Virginia

Thomas wasn't sure how the kid did it, but he managed to produce two fake IDs with access cards to get into Goldenrod's building. He also came up with two janitorial uniforms for the service they used every night. The cleaning crew showed up at midnight to start their rounds and usually finished by four in the morning.

Harold also had blueprints of the building that showed where every security camera was positioned. Thomas was amazed at how well the kid knew the building. It did nothing to alleviate his suspicions. He had more questions than ever about him.

Harold rolled out the blueprints on Thomas's kitchen table that evening. With a black felt tip marker, he circled all the security cameras.

"These are the cameras. One on every floor covering every inch of the building. The access cards will get us into the building with no problem. The second floor is where most of the research is done so we'll be out of sight." Harold flipped the page to the first level. "This is the loading dock area. And here is where the cleaning crew enters every night." He pointed to a door next to the loading dock. "That's where we'll enter."

"Are you sure this is going to work?" Thomas was already nervous and they hadn't even left yet.

"I'm not sure about anything, Tom."

It was the first time Harold had shortened his name. It surprised him. "Okay, *Harry.*"

The kid scowled. "Don't call me Harry."

"Then don't call me Tom. No one calls me that. Not even my mother."

"And no one calls me Harry."

"Now that we have that settled. Where are these VR goggles?" Thomas asked.

"In the storage room located on the first floor. I understand they were stashed inside a tub with Christmas decorations." He pointed to the storage room on the west end of the building.

"You know this for certain?"

"Unless someone discovered them and moved it, yes. And since we're still six months away from Christmas, I doubt they've been discovered. No one knows to look there," Harold said.

He sounded awfully sure of himself.

"The plan is simple," Harold continued. "We park the car just outside the employee parking lot. Which is also under surveillance."

"I know. I used to work there," Thomas said.

He ignored his jab. "We'll go in with the cleaning service and make our way to the west end of the building to the storage room. We'll grab the goggles and then get out the same way. In and out. No one will even know we're there."

Thomas inhaled a deep breath, exhaled. "I hope you're right about this."

The last thing they needed was to get caught by Janus Force. Or, worse, killed.

"Trust me." The kid flashed a bright smile.

It was not the perfect plan, but it was the only one they had. Thomas knew they were going to get caught just as he knew they were going to be arrested.

"Ready?" Harold asked.

"As I'll ever be."

Harold was certain they would be able to get in and out of Goldenrod without detection.

He hoped the kid was right.

Thomas drove. His nerves were on high alert and he was too stressed to let the kid drive. Instead of driving his beat-up pick-up, he asked Nick if he could borrow one of his vehicles. When he questioned him about why, Thomas had to come up with a plausible excuse. He said he needed the car for a quick errand in the morning and that his truck wouldn't start. Nick seemed to buy the story.

It was the only part of the situation he could control. He parked the car one block down from the employee parking lot under a tree that would give them plenty of concealment away from all the street lights. Harold deemed it perfect.

They exited the car, both dressed in their cleaning service gear. Harold picked up the pace as they headed to the back of the building where the loading dock was. Sure enough, the cleaning crew had just arrived and were unloading their company van.

"Wait," Harold whispered. "Let them all get inside first."

"Why?" Thomas asked.

"Because if we don't, they'll wonder who we are and question it."

"Good point."

They waited behind a retaining wall, peering over the edge and watching as the last person entered the building and the door slammed shut. That's when it was time to make their move. Harold vaulted over the retaining wall with his youthful ability while it took Thomas a few more minutes to climb over.

They headed down the slope and into the paved yard behind the building. At the door, Harold swiped his access card and yanked open the door. Thomas, with his heart in his throat, followed him through the door.

They were in a long, well-lit hallway. He hadn't been to this part of the building ever, so Thomas wasn't sure what to expect. It was nothing more than white walls and tile flooring. Somewhere in the distance, they could hear the *squeak, squeak, squeak* of wheels and knew the cleaning crew was somewhere up ahead.

"This way," Harold said and took off down the hall.

At a juncture, he turned left. He seemed to know exactly where he was going. Thomas questioned why he bothered to come at all if the kid knew where he was going and what he was doing. And then he reminded himself he had promised Nick he would keep an eye on him. Even if that meant breaking and entering into Goldenrod.

They wound their way through hallways, past darkened offices for security and other personnel. No one was about. The only sound was that of a vacuum in one of the offices.

"The storage room is up ahead," Harold said, his voice low. He nodded to a closed door.

When they arrived, it was marked with a brown nameplate that simply read STORAGE in big letters. Harold dropped to one knee and pulled a lock picking set from his pocket. A few seconds later, the door was open.

"You know how to pick locks?" Thomas asked, surprised.

"I know how to do a lot of things," the kid said as he pushed open the door to darkness.

When Thomas was inside, he closed the door and flipped on the light. The storage room was floor to ceiling gray metal racks stuffed full of junk. Harold went right to the back and pulled down the tub of Christmas decorations. Like he knew exactly where it was, too.

This seemed all too convenient for Thomas.

Harold yanked off the lid, stuck his hand inside the tub and came out with a small nondescript cardboard box. There was a look of triumph on his face.

"That's it?" Thomas asked.

"Yep. Let's go."

He was already replacing the lid and shoving the tub and onto the shelf. He snatched the box and stuck it under his arm. He cracked the door and peered into the hallway.

"All clear."

Thomas followed, the door closing behind them with a snap. They hurried down the hallway, rounded the corner and stopped short. Two security guards were at the other end headed for them with guns drawn and pointed at them. Thomas swore under his breath.

This was not good.

But Harold's footsteps didn't even falter when he took an immediate right turn and headed up another hallway. Thomas followed him, worried the security guards were going to follow.

"We better hurry," Harold said. "I know another way out of here."

About the time he said it, the men rounded the corner. One of them shouted. "Stop!"

"Run," Harold said.

Clutching the box, he took off down the hall. Thomas didn't have a choice but to follow him, his heart beating a wild tattoo. As he wondered what was stopping the men from shooting, a gunshot rang out. They both ducked, as if that would make the bullet miss them. Harold glanced back.

"You okay?"

"Fine," Thomas said through clenched teeth.

Harold paused at a door at the end of the hallway and flung it open. He ushered Thomas inside and slammed the door, twisting the lock. It wouldn't hold them for long.

"This is a dead end. What are we doing here?" Thomas asked.

"Trust me."

Harold handed the box with the goggles off to Thomas. He dragged a chair to the middle of the room and stood on it, shoving open a ceiling tile.

"What are you doing?" Thomas demanded.

"It's the only way. Come on."

The kid hoisted his body into the ceiling, situated himself and then turned back to Thomas. He held his hand down for the goggles. Thomas handed them up.

"I'm going to regret this," he muttered as he climbed into the chair.

Harold helped him up into the ceiling. They had just replaced the tile when they heard the door bang open. Thomas held his breath and waited. A long deathly silence followed. Then the door opened and closed again.

Harold jerked his head in a nod to follow him. They crawled through the building, the kid muttering something under his breath the whole way. He came to a halt and lifted one of the ceiling tiles off. Fluorescent lighting flooded the crawlspace. The kid wasted no time as he jumped down to the floor below.

Thomas peered over the edge. It was the hallway they had entered initially next to the loading dock. He couldn't believe it. He tossed the box down to Harold and then joined him in the hall.

"How in the world did you know about the crawlspace and how to get back here?" he asked.

A knowing smile crossed his face. "I know a lot about this building. Let's get out of here before they realize we're gone."

Harold flung open the door and they fled into the night.

# # #

*Skye and Dane's adventure will continue in
Volume 5: Sword of Vengeance*

Don't miss any of Skye and Dane's Adventures!

Highland Fling, Volume 1

A girl, a hit man and a time machine may be more than Dane Fortune can handle.

"…characters with real chemistry and a rip-roaring adventure." —5 stars, Amazon Reviewer

"…a fun twist to time travel…" —4 stars, Amazon Reviewer

"Dane Fortune is a delicious blend of everything you want in a hero." —4 stars, BookBub Reviewer

"I liked the set up for this book. It's pretty exciting and I didn't want to put it down." —5 stars, Amazon Reviewer

Dead of Winter, Volume 2

At the mercy of a faulty time machine, will Skye and Dane be able to make it home alive?

"…heart-stopping…full of anxiety-inducing moments and nail-biting suspense." —5 stars, BookBub Reviewer

"…a fun adventure that will leave [you] wanting more Ransom and Fortune." —4 stars, Amazon Reviewer

"…you'll want book 1 first so you can join in the wild ride from the beginning." —5 stars, BookBub Reviewer

"Adding the element of time travel to a book already rife with fantastical events—the story's endless possibilities are spellbinding." —Fort Worth Magazine

The Citadel, Volume 3

Still lost in time, Skye and Dane face their most dangerous enemy yet.

"What an amazing and addicting series!" —5 stars, Amazon Reviewer

"... plenty of action and a great storyline kept me reading until I finished it!" —5 stars, Amazon Reviewer

"Can't wait for the next one!" —5 stars, Amazon Reviewer

Lord of the Underworld, Volume 4

This title has never been published before and is a brand new adventure!

"This was a fast paced read…" —4 stars, Amazon Reviewer

"…a fast paced time travel adventure that is such a fun and easy read." —5 stars, Amazon Reviewer

"…a well written story that kept me turning pages, I want to read the next book." —4 stars, BookBub Reviewer

Watch for more adventures with Skye and Dane!
www.MichelleMiles.net

Praise for the Dragon Protectors

***Desiring the Dragon Lord,* Book 1**

"Michelle Miles kicks off her new Dragon Protectors series with a bang…" —4 stars, Amazon Reviewer

"I read this book in just a couple of days. I couldn't put it down!" —5 stars, Amazon Reviewer

"…a wonderful book full of strong minded characters." —5 stars, Amazon Reviewer

***Seducing the Dragon Knight,* Book 2**

"From the start this book has danger and a bit of mystery." —4 stars, Amazon Reviewer

"I love this author and this genre. A must read." —5 stars, Booksprout Reviewer

"I was half in love with Rafe when we met him in Desiring the Dragon Lord, but oh get me a fan and a cool drink, because his hot factor increased 100-fold in the second installment." —4 stars, Amazon Reviewer

***Tempting Her Dragon Bodyguard,* Book 3**

"I loved reading this book and hope there are more to come." —5 stars, Amazon Reviewer

"Book three in the Dragon Protectors series a well written story that kept me turning pages. I had to know what was going to happen." —5 stars, Amazon Reviewer

"…a captivating storyline…" —4 stars, Amazon Reviewer

Praise for Age of Wizards

In the Tower of the Wizard King, Book 1

"The book has a very strong and intriguing plotline as well as unforgettable characters. I liked the parallel narration of the present and the past as it made the story both more complicated and more involving…" —5 stars, Amazon Reviewer

"The mix of past and present stories brings the reader full circle and will keep you engrossed in the story. Beware though, you may not want to put the book down! …two thumbs up…!"

—5 stars, Goodreads Reviewer

"Michelle Miles brilliantly weaves twists and turns, love stories both past and present, secrets, betrayal and revenge, with multi-dimensional characters, two different timelines and two different worlds." —5 stars, Amazon Reviewer

"I thoroughly enjoyed every aspect of this book, and highly recommend it. Filled with fantasy and three dimensional characters I couldn't put it down." —5 stars, Amazon Reviewer

On the Hunt for the Wizard King, Book 1

"We really got to watch all of the characters grow and change throughout the book. No one was what you expected. Miles did a great job of keeping you guess and wondering what was around the next corner." —5 stars, Amazon Reviewer

"Wow! This story is so full of magic with action and adventure I could not put it down. The land of fae is an exciting magical world where anything can happen, and I definitely was not expecting some of the twist and turns that transpired."

—5 stars, Amazon Reviewer

Also by Michelle Miles

Dream Walker
Call of the Dark

Age of Wizards
In the Tower of the Wizard King
On the Hunt for the Wizard King

A Ransom & Fortune Adventure
Highland Fling, Vol 1
Dead of Winter, Vol 2
The Citadel, Vol 3
Lord of the Underworld, Vol 4

Dragon Protectors
Desiring the Dragon Lord
Seducing the Dragon Knight
Tempting Her Dragon Bodyguard

Realm of Honor
One Knight Only
Only for a Knight
A Knight to Remember
A Knight Like No Other
Shadows of the Knight

Guardians of Atlantis
Tempting Eden
Seducing Eve
Ravishing Helene
Guardians of Atlantis Box Set

Coffee House Chronicles
Talk Dirty to Me
Nice Girls Do
Have Yourself a Merry Little Latte
Take Me I'm Yours
Sex, Lust & Martinis

Forever Yours
A Little Taste of Heaven

Shorts and Anthologies
A Dance Among the Faeries, Short Story
Eorwulf, Short Story
The Soul of Sharah, Short Story
Sinfully Sweet, Short Story
Flights of Fantasy: A Collection of Short Stories

Watch for more at www.MichelleMiles.net

About the Author

Michelle Miles believes in fairy tales, true love and magic. She is the award-winning author of the epic fantasy, IN THE TOWER OF THE WIZARD KING, as well as the fantasy romance series, REALM OF HONOR, featuring knights and their ladies fair, and the paranormal dragon-shifter romance series, DRAGON PROTECTORS.

In her spare time, she enjoys listening to music, reading, cross-stitching and watching movies. Even though she's a native Texan, she loves castles, dragons, fairies and elves and is an avid Game of Thrones fan. She can be found online at Facebook, Twitter, Instagram, Pinterest, and Goodreads.

www.ingramcontent.com/pod-product-compliance
Lightning Source LLC
Chambersburg PA
CBHW071536100726
47908CB00004B/1410